WHEN A COWBOY LOVES A WOMAN

by
MAGGIE CARPENTER

ADULT ADVISORY

THIS BOOK IS FOR ADULTS only. It contains scenes of spanking, graphic sex, bondage, sensory deprivation, and are fantasies intended for adults. This book is not for children, nor does it condone corporal punishment of children. This book does not support nonconsensual spanking or any other nonconsensual activities, sexual or otherwise.

Visit Maggie Carpenter
http://www.MaggieCarpenter.com
https://www.facebook.com/MaggieCarpenterWriter

CHAPTER ONE

BRIDGET STARED OUT the window at the approaching signs of life. After three hours on the road the bus was nearing the outskirts of the small town. It had seemed like three days, and felt far away, very far away. The paperwork had warned there was no internet, and cell service was spotty at best, but that's what had sold her. It was exactly what she wanted. A place where Caden couldn't find her, and he wouldn't be able to reach her. What better place than a dude ranch in the middle of nowhere?

Pulling a scrap of paper from her pocket, she read the instructions for the umpteenth time. She had no desire to make a mistake and find herself waiting in the wrong place.

Second stop once you're in the town. Corner of Elm and Fifth. Wait outside Billy's Diner for a white van. Driver's name is Ed.

Returning her eyes to the window, she saw some modest but well kept homes. As the bus slowed down and rolled to a stop, she knew she'd soon be out on the street waiting for her ride. Landing the job was a Godsend, and she hoped she'd be able to thank the person who had referred her.

The Application For Employment had arrived uninvited, waiting in her mailbox when she'd returned from the barn late one night. She worked as an assistant trainer, though her boss was constantly away at horse shows, and new clients often thought Bridget was the one in charge. Tired and suffering from a broken heart, the contents of the elegant envelope was a sprinkle of sunshine in the grey sadness that had become her life.

"Word has reached us that you are an exceptional horse handler and trainer. We are seeking a qualified individual for the summer, with the possibility of long term employment for the right candidate."

There had been a three page, full color brochure enclosed. It was called, Dudley's Dude Ranch, and she'd pondered the name. The exquisite facility offering horse back riding, tennis, a magnificent pool area, and first class accommodations, wasn't like any dude ranch she'd ever seen. As tired as she was, she'd immediately sat down and filled out the questionnaire, enclosed some photographs of herself riding, and sent it off the following morning. When the call came in just four short days later, and the owner, Richard Tate, had offered her the position, she was overjoyed.

Caden!

She could finally escape running into Caden, hearing Caden's voice mails, and seeing his text messages.

Caden was a horse-trader and trainer. An important, successful horse-trader and trainer, but he was also a cowboy who had a reputation for being a ladies-man, and the minute she'd laid eyes on him she could see why.

Blue eyes blazed from under dark brown hair that fell in shaggy layers around his head. A physique that came from riding and working with horses every day, and thick lips that offered a crooked smile, one that gave him a wicked, playful look, but it was his demeanor that tied up his package into one crazy, hot, compelling cowboy.

HE OOZED CONFIDENCE. It was tinged with arrogance, but on Caden it only made him more alluring. That, and the fact that no woman had been able to pin him down, had made him the mouth-watering candy that all the girls wanted. Against the advice of her friends, she'd dated him, and she had fallen hard. As predicted, and to her fury, he'd broken her heart.

As the bus pulled back on to the road, Bridget swallowed the hot lump at the back of her throat. That's how it happened. She'd be perfectly fine, Caden the furthest thing from her mind, then, boom! A wave of emotion, and heavy tears threatening to break. Clenching her fists, she grit her teeth and refused to succumb.

She was glad to be getting away. There'd be no more jumping every time the phone rang, or disappointed there were no emails from him.

"By the time I leave here I'll be cured," she murmured under her breath. "Distance, that's what I need. Miles, and plenty of them. Who knows, maybe there'll be a hot, sexy cowboy at Dudley's Dude Ranch waiting to sweep me off my feet."

The bus traveled at a slow pace, too slow for Bridget. She was aching to get off. Her shoulders hurt, her back hurt, and the air in the coach was stale. The granola bars she'd brought for the journey had been consumed, but if she ever saw another one again it would be too soon. She wanted real food and a decent cup of coffee.

There were only a few passengers left, and grabbing the seat in front of her for support, she stood up and stared out the wide front windows of the bus. The main street was just ahead, and flopping back down she pulled her sweater from her large hobo bag and threw it around her shoulders. It was late in the day, the sun was setting, and though she'd brought several jackets they were packed away in her suitcase. The bus began to slow, and staring out her window she saw the diner. It was her stop.

"Thank goodness," she muttered. "I didn't think I'd ever get here."

Doing a last minute check to make sure she had everything, she zipped up her bag and let out a heavy breath. Three months to find herself, three months of nothing but horses and open spaces, three months of peace. Three months of a Caden-free zone. Climbing off the bus, she stood patiently as the driver pulled her bag from the luggage compartment.

"You sure this is the right stop?" he asked as he placed the suitcase next to her.

"Positive. I'm going to step into the diner for something to eat before my ride gets here."

"Take it easy, nice havin' you on board."

"Thanks," she said with a smile.

Turning around she studied the diner. Like most, bench seats lined the window, so leaving her suitcase where she could watch it, stretching her arms above her head as she walked, she pushed through the door and moved inside. The delicious aroma of fresh baked pies was wafting through the air, and finding the restaurant virtually empty, she didn't wait to be seated, but walked directly to the booth with the best view of the street.

"What can I getcha?"

Looking up she saw a middle-aged woman with orange hair and a large smile.

"Pie, some kind of pie," Bridget replied, "and coffee. I'll bet you have great coffee."

"We don't get many complaints," the woman smiled.

"I'd like to pay for this now. I'm expecting a ride and I'll have to bolt when it arrives."

"Sure, here you go," the waitress replied scribbling out a check and placing it on the table.

Bridget watched her head back to the kitchen, and pulling some dollars from her wallet she left enough to cover the total, along with a hefty tip. Tired from the tedious journey she felt a yawn coming on, and leaned back against the back of the bench seat. Picking up the menu, she began to browse while keeping a watchful eye on her suitcase, and as she read through the entrees, she wanted to try them all.

"Man, this looks good," she muttered eyeing the photographs of chicken fried steak, cheeseburgers, and chicken and dumplings.

"Here you go, hon."

Bridget smiled as the waitress place a deep bowl with a large helping of apple pie in front of her.

"Wow, that smells amazing," she exclaimed.

"Your coffee," the waitress continued taking a mug off her tray, "and here's a dish of vanilla ice cream on the house to welcome you to town."

"Thanks, that's so kind. I'm Bridget."

"I'm Ruby. Yes, it's the hair. I was told I arrived on this earth with a huge mess of red hair, so they had no choice but to call me Ruby."

"What a great story," Bridget laughed. "Thanks, this looks great."

"I'll leave you to it. Hope you get to finish before your ride gets here."

Slicing her fork through the crisp crust, she spooned it into her mouth and rolled her eyes. It tasted as good as a home-made pie straight from the oven. Finding the coffee as good as she expected, she downed it quickly, and half-way through her pie and ice cream, Ruby returned to refill her cup.

"Whatta ya think?" the waitress asked.

"I think this is a gold mine waiting to hit the supermarkets," Bridget replied enthusiastically.

"Glad you like it. Jeb, that's the owner and cook, he makes everything himself."

"Tell Jeb he has a new fan."

"I sure will. He loves to hear from a happy customer."

Glancing at her watch, Bridget stared down the street for any sign of the white van. It was late, not that she minded, she'd enjoyed her pie and ice-cream, but she was starting to worry. A few minutes later, as she downed her last swallow of coffee, she saw a blue and white Sheriff's car moving slowly down the block, and when it pulled up to the curb next to her suitcase, she jumped from the booth, waved a thank you and hurried out the door.

"That's mine," she called as the sheriff stepped from his car to study it.

"Not real clever, leavin' a suitcase out like that. You had folks around here worried."

"I did? I'm sorry. I just got off the bus and it was too much of a pain to lug inside the diner."

"You alone?"

"Uh, yes, my name's Bridget Cooper. I'm going to be working at Dudley's Dude Ranch. I'm just waiting for the van to pick me up."

"I hate to tell you, but you're in the wrong spot."

"What? No! I have the instructions right here," she declared, a wave of panic sweeping through her, and digging into her pocket she pulled out the small scrap of paper.

"See? It says, second stop once you're in the town. Corner of Elm and Fifth. Wait outside Billy's Diner for a white van. Driver's name is Ed."

"Miss Cooper, this isn't Billy's Diner. This is the Roadhouse Diner. The second stop is the next one, about a mile further down."

"What? No, no, no. Oh, my, God. I can't believe it. I was so anxious to get out of that stupid bus. I saw the diner and got off. I didn't think there'd be two diners in such a small town. It never even occurred to me. Oh, no, what am I going to do?"

"Most likely Ed will be gone by now. He's usually there when the bus rolls up, and it was right on time."

"Dammit," she groaned feeling the threat of frustrated tears.

"Hang on now, don't panic. I'll put your suitcase in my car and we'll go back inside. You can use their phone. We'll let them know you've arrived, and I'll take you out there."

"Seriously? Thank you, Sheriff, so much!"

"No problem. Call me Bill."

"Wow, thanks, Bill, that's so kind of you."

"It's gettin' dark. Most folks here are decent, but there are a few larrikins runnin' around. You don't wanna be standin' around on the street corner."

"But it's so calm here, so peaceful."

"Yeah, it is, but you never know. Prevention, that's better than any cure," he declared lifting her bag into the back seat of his car. "Come on, let's find out what's what."

As the sheriff had predicted, Ed had been waiting when the bus had arrived. Only one passenger got off, and it was a young man.

"I'm so sorry," she apologized.

"We're all sittin' havin' supper right now, but I'll be there soon."

"Where would you like me to wait?" she asked.

"Here, give me the phone," the Sheriff smiled.

Handing him the receiver, Bridget stood back and leaned against the wall.

"I need to make a run out there anyways," the Sheriff said. "I'll drop her off."

"That's real good of you, Bill," Ed said gratefully. "I appreciate it."

"You're welcome."

Hanging up the phone, he thanked Ruby, then walked with Bridget out to his cruiser.

"I'm so embarrassed," she mumbled. "What a way to start a new job."

"It's not the first time. They tell people, the second stop, but they should say, the second diner," he said as he opened the car door for her. "I've suggested that to them time and again."

"Really? I'm not the only who who's done this? I'm so relieved to hear that," she said climbing into the car.

"Try not to worry too much. You'll settle in. They're a nice bunch out there. They've got some real good horses, and it's a beautiful place," he remarked settling behind the wheel.

"That's what I heard. They don't have a website, so I could only go by what I was told on the phone and saw in the brochure."

"If you need anything, you call me," he grinned reaching into his breast pocket. "Here's my card."

"Bill, my Knight in a Shining Sheriff's car," she laughed. "I'm glad I left my suitcase out. It wasn't a stupid thing to do after all."

"Not this time anyway," he chuckled.

"How far is this place?" she asked as a long yawn swept through her.

"About twenty minutes. Sit back and relax. You must be tuckered out."

"Thanks, I am."

Resting her head between the door and the headrest, she closed her eyes, and though she was aware of the hum of the tires, and the occasional squawking of the sheriff's radio, she fell into a soft doze. When the car rolled over a bump and began to slow down, she blinked open her eyes.

"Are we here?"

"Yep, we are. Dudley's Dude Ranch."

Glancing out the window she saw the large, upscale two-story colonial home. Painted white and blue with three gables on the second story, it was as elegant and as impressive as the brochure had suggested. A circular driveway swept around a multi-colored lit fountain, and as Bill began rolling to a stop, a tall, lanky man stepped out the front door to meet them.

"I can't believe this place," she mumbled.

"This is a first-class operation," Bill said looking at her astonished face.

"I saw the pictures, but it's even grander than they show," she remarked as she picked up her hobo bag from the floor in front of her.

"Dudley's Dude Ranch caters to the rich and famous," Bill said. "They come out here to get away from things."

"I did know about that, it's one of the reasons I'm here, to get away, I mean, but I honestly didn't expect this."

"You'll probably be in one of the cabins out back. There are half a dozen of 'em, and they're all miniature versions of the house."

"I'm suddenly feeling a whole lot better," she smiled.

The tall lanky man opened her door, introduced himself as Ed, and as he pulled her suitcase from the back seat, she turned back to the sheriff who had rescued her.

"Bill, I owe you. Will you let me buy you dinner at the diner when I get a night off?"

"That's not necessary, I'm glad I could help."

"Thanks again," she smiled, and closing the car door she followed Ed into the house.

"Richard Tate has already retired for the evening, but he'd like you to meet him in his office at eight-thirty in the morning," Ed said, his manner polite and friendly. "If you're hungry, dinner's still on. When there are no guests the staff can eat in the dining room, otherwise you have a kitchen in your cabin."

"I had some apple pie at the diner, but yes, please, I'd love some dinner."

He led her down a hallway and through a door into a large dining room, and as a group of smiling faces looked up at her, she felt herself relax. Grinning back, she was sure she was about to enjoy a truly great summer.

CHAPTER TWO

BRIDGET FOUND HER FELLOW staff members welcoming and warm, but the other horse handlers she'd been told about, Max, the manager, Jane, who was Max's assistant, and Tim, weren't there. She decided not to stay long, wanting to be fresh for the morning, and when she reached her small cabin and was hit by a wave of exhaustion, she was glad she'd eaten and left the table quickly.

Her cabin was small but cozy, with a separate bedroom, a full bathroom, and a decent kitchen that was open to the living area and offered a counter with three bar stools. As the sheriff had mentioned, it was a miniature version of the house, but decorated in burgundy and grey.

After a long, hot shower, Bridget slipped into a cotton T-shirt and climbed into bed. The mattress was soft and forgiving, but she could feel the firm support, and closing her eyes she immediately began to fall asleep.

Most nights she dreamed about Caden, and most nights she would struggle to escape, and most nights she would win, but her fatigue was too great. When he came to life and meandered towards her, his dark brown, shaggy hair, falling over one eye, and his mesmerizing blue eyes promising to journey with her to the stars, she gave up the battle.

Waiting for the recall of his devouring hug that she missed so much, and the deep aching need that would sweep through her body, she saw herself standing in a lush paddock with her arms open. The grass was blindingly green, then suddenly she was spinning. The dizziness captured her, holding her in its clutches, and as she fought her way out of the cyclonic winds, his voice echoed through the tumult.

"When a cowboy loves a woman...when a cowboy loves a woman..."

Her body jerked as the tornado spat her out, and sitting bolt upright, breathless and sweating, she gazed around the dark, still room.

"Why are you haunting me?" she gasped. "Why can't I let you go? I hate you, I hate you so much."

Dissolving into tears she fell back on the bed and clung to the pillow. As the salty wetness spilled across her face, and the painful, gnawing void engulfed her, the memory of the moment, the one that had shattered her hopeful dreams and plunged a saber into her heart, stood bright and clear in her mind's eye.

It had been six weeks earlier, but to Bridget it still felt like yesterday. Caden had stayed the night in her modest apartment, waking her with soft kisses on her neck, his fingers lightly pinching her nipples, and his hardness pressing against her. Thrusting back, moaning her need, she had surrendered to the joy as he'd slithered into her hungry canal, and with robust strokes, and warm whispers of love, he had ridden her to an explosive, tingling, delicious climax.

She had floated through the following hours as she'd taken care of her chores around the stable, laughed with him through lunch, and later that afternoon, she'd felt his eyes on her when she'd been giving a riding lesson. She hadn't expected him to return to the barn, and she'd been thrilled to see him. He'd waved from the fence, then sauntered off towards a shiny black pickup that had rolled up the drive.

A short time later, the girl she was teaching begged to finish early, claiming she was too tired and too hot. When it stopped being fun there was no point, so they'd called it a day, and as the girl wandered away to join her mother, Bridget had led the horse, Bogart, back to the barn.

She had heard the deep, seductive voice that was uniquely his, then the wistful tones of a woman. Her pulse ticked up. She'd been warned, she'd been begged, she'd been told more times than she could remember, *don't go out with Caden. He's a cheat. He'll break your heart.*

The ground was soft beneath her feet, even the hoof falls from Bogart walking calmly behind her made little noise. It was a hot, bright day, and moving into the shadow of the barn it took a moment for her eyes to adjust. A dark-haired girl she'd not seen before, her eyes closed, was leaning against Caden's chest with her head in the crook of his shoulder. His bare muscled arms were around her, and he was stroking her hair.

Bridget froze.

She couldn't breathe.

She couldn't move.

She couldn't cry out.

It was Bogart who broke the spell. Ready for his saddle to be off, and hungry for some hay, he'd nudged her. It was a gentle push, a polite request to keep moving. Her body was shaking, tears were burning at the back of her eyes, and her stomach was wrapping itself into painful knots.

Barely able to control the desire to race across the barn and rip the girl from Caden's hold, she'd backed away into the harsh light of the sun and moved to the side of the building. A few minutes passed and the girl had left, with Caden following a minute later. Trembling, and fighting the overwhelming emotion, Bridget had quickly finished grooming Bogart, ducking out of sight whenever Caden called her name, then told the barn manager she was coming down with a migraine. Jumping in her car she'd sped to a tavern on the outskirts of town, staying there until late in the evening.

Caden had called and emailed, but she'd ignored all his attempts at contact. Two days later, when he'd finally caught her at her apartment, Bridget's deep hurt had become intense anger. She'd allowed him to enter, then exploded, hurling words at him as fast as they formed, refusing to listen to his excuses, then ordering him out she'd literally pushed him on to her front porch. She was about to slam the door when he lunged forward and put his foot against it.

"Bridget, you're makin' a big mistake. Why won't you let me explain?"

"You'll serenade me with your sweet words and you'll weave your charm right around my heart," she railed at him. "I'm not going to let you make a fool of me. No, Caden, you blew it."

"Stop yellin' at me girl, it's not what you think. If anyone's blowin' somethin' here, it's you, right now."

"Go away. I never want to see you again," she hissed. "How much clearer can I be?"

"You," he said in a harsh whisper, leaning forward and shaking his finger, "you need a good spankin'. You're bein' totally unreasonable."

"WHAT?"

"You're throwin' a tantrum."

"Fuck you, asshole!"

Kicking his shin, making him jerk back his leg, she'd slammed the door. She'd fallen back against it trying to catch her breath, but then he'd unexpectedly called something out to her, something he'd whispered in her ear several times before.

"Don't forget, Bridget, when a cowboy loves a woman..."

Those last words had stayed with her ever since, floating around her head, popping up at the oddest moments, and often echoing through her dreams.

Switching on her bedside lamp, she slipped from the sheets, and padding into the bathroom she splashed her face with cold water. Staring at her reflection, she saw bleary, red-rimmed eyes looking back at her.

"Time and distance is what you need, Bridget," she muttered, "it's the only cure. You've managed to create the distance, and in time this pain will stop."

Ambling back to bed she managed to fall asleep, and as usual, the second time around there were no dreams, just the peace of restful darkness. When the birds outside her window tweeted her awake, she rolled over and gazed at the clock on the nightstand. It was seven-forty a.m. With a yawn and a stretch she focused on the day ahead.

Having worked on dude ranches in the past, she knew what to expect. She'd be taken to the barn, introduced to the horses, their habits and idiosyncrasies explained, then put to work cleaning the tack, learning the feeding regimen, and finding her way around. This, however, was unlike any dude ranch she'd ever seen, and as she pulled on clean jeans and a shirt, she threw away her preconceptions.

Wandering into the compact kitchen hoping to find a coffee pot, she was shocked to discover the cupboards were fully stocked. Various cereals lined the shelves, along with tea and coffee, sugar, canned goods, and even a package of chocolate chip cookies. The refrigerator had all the essentials. Milk, butter, eggs, cheese, tomatoes, a lettuce and salad dressing. On the counter she found a list of everything the cabin contained, and at the bottom of the sheet, she learned she could checkmark whatever items she needed replenishing, and they'd be delivered the following day.

"This is unbelievable," she murmured as she made herself some granola and started the kettle.

After her breakfast, and two cups of coffee, she headed up the winding pathway and into the back door of the large house. She'd seen the kitchen only briefly the night before, and as she wandered in she was seriously impressed. Stainless steel gleamed at her, Viking appliances lined the walls, and hanging above the center island was a chandelier of gleaming copper pots and pans. Three people in white aprons were bustling about, but a young man with a crew cut spotted her and walked forward extending his hand.

"Hello, you must be Bridget," he said with a warm smile. "I'm Albert, the chef. This is Penny and Julia, my assistants."

The two young women nodded their greeting, then continued their chopping and mixing.

"If you run out of supplies you can always come here, but you have to check with one of us before taking anything."

"Thanks, this place is something else," she declared, "and I don't just mean this incredible kitchen."

"I've only been here six months, but I love it. The head honchos take care of the staff almost as well as they take care of their guests. They want everyone to feel appreciated. A happy staff makes for happy guests, that's what Richard says."

"I'm supposed to be meeting him right now," Bridget said checking her watch. "I'd better scurry. Can you please point me in the direction of his office?"

"Through the dining room and down the hall to your left, first door on the right. Don't worry, Richard's great. He'll make you feel welcome, and you can ask him anything. He has no problem talking about this place. He's very proud of what he's done here."

"Thanks, Albert. That's good to know. I guess I'll see you later."

In one of the few articles she had read about the ranch, it had been described as a luxury escape for those with hefty wallets. When she'd accepted the position it wouldn't have mattered if it was a weatherworn cabin. All she'd cared about was that it was far away and she could start immediately, but as she moved through the artfully decorated rooms, she realized the beauty surrounding her was good for her soul. It was uplifting and cheery, and it was making her smile.

Finding the thickly carpeted hallway, she spotted the door with a brass plaque announcing the name, Richard Tate, and gently knocked.

"Come in."

Pushing it open she stepped inside and found herself surrounded by historic art prints of the old west, and bronze sculptures of cowboys and horses. The room was forest green with white trim, and elegantly masculine.

"Bridget, such a pleasure," Richard Tate said warmly, standing up from behind his impressive desk.

He was a large man, tall, wide, and slightly overweight, and Bridget guessed him to be in his fifties.

"Mr. Tate, thanks for the opportunity. This place is beautiful."

"Thank you. We do our best. Call me Richard," he said warmly, "everyone does. Please, have a seat."

Sitting in one of the two chairs in front of the desk, she watched him settle back down, take a manila folder, and pull out a sheet of paper.

"Is your cabin all right? Is there anything you need?"

"The cabin is lovely, and I was so surprised to find all the supplies."

"We want you to be comfortable and happy here. It's important for you to be able to hibernate if you need to, and have what you need. If there's something you want just write it on the list and it will be picked up, short of caviar," he joked.

"I feel very privileged to be here. I had no idea it would be like this."

"We rarely have staff vacancies, and we're particular about who works here, and you, Bridget, came highly recommended. I'm sure you'll prove to be a valuable addition to our family."

"May I ask, how did you hear about me?"

"Through a friend of a friend," he said vaguely. "We're relaxed here, and if you have any questions don't be shy. These are the rules. They must be followed for your safety, and the safety of everyone else. Take a look at them, keep them with you for a while in case any doubts arise."

"Thank you, I'll go over them carefully," she said glancing at the list as he handed it over.

"The guests, they are the reason we're here," he continued. "They come to escape, to relax, to be with the horses or play tennis, whatever, and not worry about people bothering them. We have very little cell service, and no internet. You probably didn't see it, but there is a land-line phone in your cabin. It's in the armoire with your television."

"You have televisions here? I was exhausted when I got in last night and I went straight to bed. This morning I was so engrossed with everything I found in the kitchen, I never did get around to opening the armoire."

"Yes, we have televisions, it's a bit surprising, I know. That's the one thing the guests do not wish to be without. We have a large satellite dish behind the house up on the ridge. Do you have any questions?"

"If I want to go into town, is there a taxi service? How does that work?"

"We have several cars here, just check with Celeste, she's our general manager and her office is just a couple of doors down. I should also mention, and this will probably surprise you, I don't have much to do with the barn, that's Max's domain, so he'll go over your schedule."

"Is that where I should go now, down to the barn?"

"Today I want you to wander the grounds, move through the house, learn where everything is. Yes, of course, go to the barn, but it's important you're familiar with the entire property, inside and out, so if a guest asks you for directions, or requests something, you'll know the answer."

"I understand. Since I'm here, I'll start inside."

"We're usually solidly booked, but we close the first four days of every month for maintenance. We give the place a thorough cleaning and take care of the things we can't while we're accommodating people. You've arrived in the middle of it, which will give you plenty of time to familiarize yourself before the first guests of the month arrive."

"Good timing."

"Yes, it is. I try to plan it this way when someone new is joining us, and I'm glad it worked out that way for you. Tomorrow the trainer we use to keep us supplied with horses is coming in."

"You switch out horses?"

"We can have a dozen horses here comfortably, but we own twice that many. Our regular guests have their favorites and they request them, so he brings them in and takes others out. Sometimes a guest falls in love with a horse and wants to buy it. That happens more often than you might think."

"He must be close by to do that so often."

"His facility's about an hour from here. I understand he has about four or five cowboys working for him. Tomorrow he's bringing in several of our horses he took back there for some tuning up, along one of his own that he wants to ride on our trails. Apparently the horse is a former champion. If the trainer is open to it, would you like to try him out?"

"I'd love it," she beamed. "What's his name?"

"Valentino. His former owner named him. He was her pet, according to Caden."

"S,sorry, did you say, Caden?" she asked, her heart leaping out of her chest and landing on the desk in front of her.

"Yes, Caden Price. He's about the best horseman I ever met, not that I've met that many," he chuckled. "I guess that about wraps it up. Lunch is served at noon. I'd like you to be there so I can officially welcome you."

"Yes, thanks, Richard. I'll see you there."

Slowly rising from her chair, her pulse pounding in her temples, Bridget turned and walked from the room, her mind racing.

No! No! How could this have possibly happened? Caden? Coming here? Tomorrow? This is a bad dream, it has to be. Fuck!

CHAPTER THREE

LATE THE FOLLOWING morning, Caden Price rolled the horse van down the long, picturesque driveway into Dudley's Dude Ranch. He'd been unable to settle the nervous rumbling in his stomach through the hour-long drive, and as the large, two-story, familiar colonial house came into view, he found himself doubting what he'd done.

"Maybe this was a huge mistake," he muttered, "but I can't let her go on thinkin' I'd messed around. I can't. I have to get through to her. Such a stubborn girl, though, geez."

Driving past the house and following the road down to the stables, Caden saw Max waiting for him, along with a couple of the grooms. As usual the place was immaculate, and slowly pulling to a stop he glanced at the monitor above his head. The camera inside the van gave him constant surveillance of his precious cargo, and they all looked well and happy.

"Hey, Max, everything okay?" he asked through his open window.

"Yep, no problems. I hear you're stayin' overnight," Max remarked.

"I think so," Caden replied as he jumped from the cab. "It's been a while since I've had a break, and I couldn't think of any place better than this."

"You got that right," Max grinned. "Let's take a look at this new boy you were tellin' me about."

"He's a beauty, and a real gentleman."

Opening the doors and lowering the ramp, the two men moved inside and began unloading the horses, handing them off to the grooms at the bottom of the ramp. Valentino, though, Caden kept, and lightly holding the lead rope he walked the horse around, watching the handsome chestnut lift his nose in the air and whinny.

"That's a real nice lookin' horse," Max said admiring the muscled, gleaming, copper-coated gelding.

"So easy to ride, real smooth, and nothin' bothers him. Just a treat. I picked him up from a girl who's headin' off to college overseas. Broke her heart to let him go, but she'll be able to visit him when she wants. Most important thing for her was findin' him the best home she could. I was real complimented when she said that was me."

"Why'd you bring him here? Does Richard wanna buy him?"

"No, I promised her I wouldn't sell him, and I'm gonna keep my word. He's just had a tough time adjustin'. I swear he's missin' her. I thought maybe a change of scenery might help."

"Don't you think that might unsettle him more?"

"Maybe, or maybe it will help snap him out of it. Get his mind off things, like it helps us humans sometimes."

"What's his name again?"

"Valentino, and I used to see how he and Melinda, that's the girl who had to leave, I used to see how they were together. He was a real Romeo with her."

During their dialogue, the horse had been eyeing his new surroundings, sniffing the air, and taking a few agitated steps.

"What do you plan to do with him while you're here?" Max asked.

"I wanna ride him on some of the trails you have. Like I said, just a change for him."

"Let's put him in a pasture," Max suggested. "Let him have a walk around, eat some grass."

"Sounds good," Caden agreed.

"You'll never guess who's arrivin' tomorrow?" Max said with a spark in his eye as they headed across the stable yard to the paddocks.

"With the folks that show up here, I can't even begin to guess," Caden chuckled.

"Hold on to your hat, cowboy. Heather Chadwick."

"No shit. Heather Chadwick," Caden repeated letting out a low whistle. "I think I'll be stickin' around an extra night."

"I thought you might say that," Max chuckled. "I hear she's comin' alone. She and that rocker, what's-his-name..."

"Jeff Ludlow?"

"Yeah, Jeff Ludlow, I heard their engagement fell apart. I'm guessin' she's comin' here 'cos of that. You know, a break from the tabloids, the drama."

"A place to heal her heart," Caden mumbled, *like Bridget.*

"What did you just say?" Max asked as he opened the gate to the large, green paddock.

"I said, she's comin' here to heal her heart," Caden replied.

"Poetic," Max grinned, "and probably right on the money."

Walking Valentino into the pasture while Max waited at the gate, Caden talked to him, then offered him a carrot as he slowly removed the halter. The horse looked around, took a few steps, then began trotting away. The horses in the adjacent fields began whinnying their welcome, running up to the fence to meet the visitor.

"I'm gonna walk on up to the house and see Richard, then grab me some coffee," Caden said as he ambled back to the gate.

"I'll have the guys clean out the van," Max offered. "You got anything in there you want me to put away?"

"Thanks, Max, sure. The saddle and bridle for Valentino, it's the only thing in the front compartment."

"I'll see to it," Max assured him, then looking at the chestnut gelding who had begun bucking and playing, he shook his head and smiled. "He's a stunner."

"Yep, he is. I'll be back, thanks again."

Caden started to walk up the drive. His stomach was still churning, and though he knew what he wanted to say to Bridget, as he ran the words through his head for the umpteenth time, he shook his head and stared at the ground in dismay.

It sounds like a speech, hollow, not real. Man, this is tough. I love that she's such a spitfire, but right now I just need her to sit still and listen. How the heck am I gonna manage that? Richard will have told her I was comin' by now, so maybe she'll have wrapped her brain around it long enough to-

"What the hell are you doing here?"

Her voice shocked him, and snapping up his head, darting his eyes around, he searched her out.

"Behind you," she said testily. "You're lucky I don't have a fucking gun, or I'd be happy to shoot you in the back, though a knife would be better, yeah, a knife to stab you in the back, the same knife you used on me."

Taking a breath, Caden turned slowly around, his heartbeat ticking up as he stared at her. In the six weeks they'd been apart it was obvious she'd been in the sun. Her tanned skin made her green eyes pop, and her auburn hair had streaks of sun-kissed blond.

"Hey, Bridget, you look fantastic," he said calmly. "I'm so happy to see you."

"Well, I'm not happy to see you. Why are you here?"

"I, uh, just delivered some horses," he replied. *I don't wanna lie to you. I wanna tell you I'm here to see you, but you're still as mad as a hornet. I guess I'd better ask you the same question.* "What about you? Why are you here?"

"I'm working here, at least for the summer, not that it's any of your business," she snapped.

"Bridget, please, stop with the temper. I'd really like-"

"Let's get this straight. I have a right to my temper, it's justified. I don't know how long you'll be here, but stay the fuck out of my way, got it?"

"Sure, I've got it, Miss Potty Mouth," he said with a deep frown.

"What did you just say?" she demanded, her eyes blazing.

"You can be as mad as you want, but honey, usin' that word, you know it makes me wanna whack your butt."

"Fuck, fuck, fuck," she hissed. "Now stay the FUCK out of my way!"

Watching her turn on her heel and march away, he wanted to kick himself.

"Dammit, why did I say that?" he mumbled dropping his eyes. "Of all the things to come out of my mouth, that was the reddest flag I could've waved at her. Dammit."

Sighing heavily, he turned and continued his journey up to the house, and as he walked through the door, the cool air-conditioning hit him. Pausing to take in a grateful breath, Celeste, the woman Richard referred to as the general manager, though she thought the title a tad glorified, hurried up to greet him.

"Hi Caden, how are you?"

"Hey, Celeste, I'm hot and tired and in need of coffee," he declared.

"Come on in and I'll fetch you some, and something to eat. How does a salmon salad sandwich sound?"

"That sounds outstandin'," he nodded.

"Aren't you staying the night?" she asked as she walked with him into the large dining room.'

"I'm plannin' on it, I'd like to stay two nights if there's room."

"There's always room for you, Caden, even if I have to put a bunk bed in the storage closet," she laughed. "The only reason I asked is because you don't have a bag."

"Damn, I left it in the truck," he grunted. "My mind was wrapped up in other things."

"You go and wash your hands. You look done in, you poor man. I'll arrange your food and get your bag up here."

"That's real sweet of you, Celeste. Thanks"

"Is it in the front of the cab?"

"Yep, sittin' on the passenger seat. I feel foolish, leavin' it like that."

"We had a new girl start yesterday, pretty thing, sweet as could be. Apparently an excellent rider and handler. You two should have a lot in common. I'll page her to bring it up. She needs to get used to running around. You know how our guests can be."

"Not personally, but I can imagine," Caden remarked, not sure how he felt about Bridget doing the errand.

"I've put you in 107, may as well give you this now," Celeste said taking a large brass key from her pocket and handing it to him. "It's the closest to the paddocks. I know how you like to watch the horses."

"Thanks so much, Celeste. I'm gonna duck my head in and say hi to Richard after I wash up, then I'll be right back."

"Are you sure you don't want some coffee first?"

"I do, but I also wanna sit and enjoy it," he replied.

"I understand that feeling," she said with a wide smile. "The sandwich will be ready when you get back."

Wishing he could simply plonk himself down at the dining room table, he entered the elegant men's room off the foyer, washed up and ran his fingers through his hair, then walked down the hallway to Richard Tate's office.

Caden considered Richard a dear friend far more than a long-time client. When the plush ranch was starting up, Richard had taken a chance on him, even though he was young and just starting out. Over the years they'd developed a trusting and close relationship, and had become more like father and son than business colleagues. Knocking on the office door, he waited until Richard called him in. He knew it wasn't necessary, but he liked giving Richard the respect.

"Hey, you don't have to knock, Caden. I keep telling you that."

"The one time I don't, I'll interrupt somethin' important," Caden said with a grin.

"You look-"

"Yeah, done in. Celeste just told me," Caden said with his famously crooked smile. "She's rustlin' me up some coffee and a snack."

"I don't think it's lack of coffee or food that's making you look like that. There's only one reason for your face to be so crinkled, and her name is Bridget."

"You got that right," Caden said flopping into the same chair Bridget had sat in the day before.

"I take it you've already bumped into her," Richard said leaning across his desk.

"Yep. Walkin' up here, but I wasn't ready. She took me by surprise, and of course, I opened my mouth and inserted my foot."

"You didn't tell her it was you who arranged the job here!"

"No, no, not quite that bad."

"Then what? You don't have to tell me, but I can't help being curious."

"When we were together, if she got real upset about somethin', she'd use the 'f' word, and I'd scold her, or give her a swat, playful like, but I meant it. I don't like girls cussin'. She was mad as heck when she saw me, and she told me to stay the 'f' outta her way."

"Uh-oh, and you said?"

"I told her the truth, that I didn't like it, and it made me wanna smack her butt."

"Caden, that's not exactly the way to a girl's heart."

"Probably not, and it probably doesn't help that one of the last things I said to her when we broke up was that she needed a good spankin', and she does, dammit. I still hold to that, and I'll tell her so if I ever get the chance."

"If you want my advice, you'll send her flowers and chocolates, and romance her with gifts, then beg her to listen, not threaten bodily harm."

In spite of his frustration, Caden laughed out loud.

"Bodily harm, I think that's what she wants to do to me. You might be right. Anyway, I just wanted to say hi, let you know I was here. Valentino is in the middle paddock opposite the stable if you wanna see him. I'm gonna take him out this afternoon for a ride."

"I took a chance and suggested to Bridget that she could have the privilege of riding him. I know he's not staying, but I thought it might give you two a chance to spend some time together."

"Hey, Richard, that's great. Thanks. If you have any more brilliant ideas, please tell me. Flowers, huh, didn't think of it, maybe I'll give that a try."

"You've never sent a girl flowers?"

"Plenty of times, but at the start, you know, in my pre-Bridget days when I had a revolving front door."

"You're paying for your sins," Richard remarked raising his eyebrows.

"Yep, I guess I am, and now, if you don't mind, I'm gonna go have me some coffee and a sandwich."

"You go ahead, though we will be having lunch at midday, and she'll definitely be there."

"So will I," Caden said rising from his chair. "You can count on it."

Moving quickly back to the dining room, he found a place had been set for him, and a carafe of coffee was waiting. Splashing it into the mug and adding the sugar and cream, he took several long swallows, then letting out a breath he topped it up.

Sitting alone in the empty, quiet room, he started to feel restless, and rising to his feet he stepped across to the window. As he glanced into the driveway, he saw Bridget walking towards the house carrying his bag. His first impulse was to run out and take it from her, but he stopped himself.

It's not heavy. No, I think I'll let you deliver it to me. You'll have to keep a civil tongue bringing it in here. Maybe I can have a half-way decent conversation with you.

"Caden, your food is here."

Turning around he saw Julie, one of the chef's assistants, place the sandwich on the table mat.

"Thanks, I'm starvin'."

"I didn't make it too big, we've going to serve a serious lunch today. Albert still has some new dishes he needs to test for the next lot of guests that are due to arrive. That sandwich is one of them."

"Great. Talk about timing," he said as he returned to the table and sat down.

"Tonight too. If you can stay for dinner you should."

"Oh, I am, I'm stayin' both tonight and tomorrow."

"Excellent. Just give a yell if you need anything."

"No, I will not give a yell," he said raising an eyebrow, "I'll poke my head in."

"Whatever works," Julie laughed. "I hope you like it."

"It looks great, I know I will. Thanks."

As Julie left the room, Caden took a bite of the sandwich and nodded his head.

Man this is good. I could eat a dozen of these, no problem.

"What do you mean, you'll be staying here two nights?"

Her voice had been a whisper, and still chewing, Caden raised his eyes and looked up. Bridget had his bag in her hands, and was standing at the opposite end of the table glowering at him. Slowly placing his sandwich back on his plate, he picked up his napkin, wiped his hands, then the corners of his mouth.

"Is that my bag?" he asked ignoring her question.

"You know it is," she spat. "Two nights? You're staying here two nights?"

"Could you bring it here please?"

He could see she was about to snap something back at him, but Celeste walked into the room, stopping her cold.

"Ah, Bridget, I see you've met Caden, our handsome cowboy. Thanks for fetching that for him."

"My pleasure," Bridget said forcing a smile.

"Would you mind bringing it over?" Caden repeated. *Look at you. You want to throw it at me. I do admire your self-control, Bridget. I wish you'd exert some of that when I'm trying to talk to you.*

"Sure," she said quietly, and walking slowly towards him, her eyes never left his. "Here you are."

Caden studied her as she placed it next to his chair. She was still staring at him, and there was something in her Mona Lisa smile that sent a prickle to the back of his neck.

What are you up to, Bridget Cooper? I know that look.

"Bridget, I'm going to have a cup of coffee with Caden while he eats. Would you like to join us?"

"Oh, thank you, but no. I have to run back to the barn. Max is waiting to go over some things with me."

"We'll see you at lunch then," Celeste smiled.

"Yes, you will," she replied, and with a last look at Caden, she ambled from the room.

As Caden watched her walk away, his radar began to beep.

"You are definitely up to something," he muttered. "That was a flicker of wickedness in your eyes just now. I'll need to keep my eyes open. The mood you're in, there could be a rattlesnake in my bag."

CHAPTER FOUR

AFTER FINISHING HIS coffee and snack, Caden picked up his overnight bag and made his way up the stairs to his suite. All the guest rooms were suites, and equally exquisite. Working since six that morning he wanted to take a shower, kick up his feet and take a quick nap, and as he unlocked the door he welcomed the sight of the beautifully appointed room. Horses and dirt were in his blood, but that didn't impede his appreciation for living well. Moving into the bedroom he placed his bag on the bench at the foot of the bed, then wandered across to the window to look down on the paddocks below. What he saw surprised and delighted him.

Bridget was in the paddock with Valentino, and the big gelding had his head buried in her chest. She was stroking his neck, and he could see the horse was putty in her hands. While Valentino had been well behaved and no trouble, Caden hadn't seen him demonstrate such affection with anyone except Melinda.

For the first two weeks after she'd left, the horse been anxious and depressed. Caden had loaded him into the van and trailered him from his in-town training and sales facility where he'd been boarded, to his large, sprawling ranch. The wide open spaces seemed to help, but he still wasn't the happy horse he'd been under Melinda's care. Staring down at Bridget, seeing the horse wanting to crawl into her lap, filled his heart with relief and joy.

"You do have a way about you, Bridget. Look at that, he adores you. I know how he feels," Caden mumbled.

As Bridget walked away, Valentino followed her, and when she began to run, the gelding trotted next to her, playfully tossing his head. Caden continued to watch the interaction, then feeling the weariness seep into his bones he walked into the bathroom, stripped off, and turned on the shower. Stepping under the hot water, washing off the dust from the long morning, he pondered Richard's suggestion.

"Flowers and chocolates? There's nothin' wrong with bein' old-fashioned, hell, there's a lot right with it. If she won't talk to me, maybe I could send a letter along with the gifts explainin' what she saw, but things can get misunderstood in a letter. No. Not my style. Better to do things in person."

Drying off, he wrapped a towel around his waist, walked across to his bag for a change of clothes, and was about to open it when he recalled the look in Bridget's eyes. Convinced she'd been up to mischief, very slowly, and standing back, he pulled open the zipper. Nothing jumped out at him, and peering inside the contents appeared to be completely untouched.

Pulling on a fresh white T-shirt, he finished unpacking the few clothes he'd brought, and then it hit him. The bag was empty. His clean underwear and socks were gone.

"You brat, Bridget Cooper," he exclaimed, "I knew it!"

Staring at the bag, his hands on his hips, though he was shaking his head he couldn't help but break into a grin, and reaching for the phone he called Richard's office.

"You ready for this?"

"I don't know," Richard replied. "Am I?"

"I left my overnight bag in the van, so Celeste sent Bridget to fetch it. I just discovered she relieved it of all my underwear and socks."

"She did what?"

"You heard me."

"I like this girl," Richard chuckled. "That's brilliant."

"I wanted to wring her neck, but I have to admit I'm grinnin' as well."

"I assume you're in your room."

"Yes, Richard, I'm in my room with a towel around my waist."

"I'm sorry," Richard said chortling loudly, "but this is hilarious. Don't worry, I'll be right there."

"Thanks."

Hanging up the phone, Caden moved back to the window and stared down at the paddock. Bridget was still playing with Valentino; the horse's spirit was back, and the sight was pure magic.

"What am I gonna do now? I'm real happy to see you like that again, big fella, but what's gonna happen when I load you back into the van to take you home. One problem is solved, and it presents me with another."

A knock told him Richard had arrived, and wishing he could run down to the paddock and join Bridget and the happy horse, he walked across the room and answered the door.

"Sorry, Richard, I thought it was unlocked. Come in."

"No problem, here you go. You know what this means, don't you?"

"Yeah," Caden frowned taking the unopened packets of underwear and socks from his friend. "It means I have to borrow a car and go into town, and I was gonna take a nap."

"Besides that."

"I'm not sure, what?"

"She's engaging you. She's communicating."

Caden was already ripping open the plastic packaging around the briefs, but he paused, staring at his friend.

"Damn. You're right. I wonder if she knows that."

"She might not, but that was lifting up the sword, throwing down the gauntlet, that was an attention grabber, an invitation, a-"

"You can stop now," Caden said holding up his hand. "I get it. Damn. Hope springs eternal."

"The question is, what's your response."

"You know what I'm thinkin'?" Caden said pensively.

"I'm afraid to ask, what?"

"None. Nada. Nothin'. A kid throws a tantrum, what's the best thing to do?"

"Ignore it," Richard declared.

"Exactly. I won't say a word. When I go down to watch her ride Valentino, I won't say a word. It'll drive her nuts."

"You are a cruel man, Caden Price, and I'm not sure that's smart."

"Hey, all's fair in love and war, besides, she's got it comin'. Maybe the best way to get her attention is to stop askin' for it. Oh, by the way, speakin' of Valentino, go look out the window."

As Richard walked across the room to look down at the paddock, Caden pulled on the ill-fitting briefs and grabbed a pair of jeans.

"Two peas in a pod," Richard remarked. "Talk about a match."

"No kiddin'. That horse has been depressed ever since his owner left. That's the first time I've seen him like that. What the blazes can I do now?"

"Think on it," Richard said wisely. "That, my friend, is a bigger problem than getting Bridget to listen to you. The prank is proof of that. It's just a matter of time now."

"Yeah, I agree," Caden said slipping into a shirt. "I'm feelin' almost as happy as that horse. I never thought I'd be pleased that someone took my underwear and socks," he laughed.

"Here, take my car," Richard offered pulling the key from his pocket. "It's the silver Mercedes in the garage."

"Thanks, Richard. Do you need anythin' while I'm in town?"

"Nope. Just make sure you're back for lunch at midday."

"Are you kiddin'? I wouldn't miss it."

"Caden, before I leave..."

"Yeah, what?"

"Think twice about ignoring her."

The look on Richard's face was serious, and Caden had learned to listen to his older, wiser friend.

"Why do you say that?"

"She's given you what you want. You have her attention. In her own whacky way she's reaching out to you. You went to a lot of trouble getting her here, and it's worked, my friend. You don't want to reject her now."

"Dammit, Richard, you're right," Caden sighed. "How could I not see that? I was about to be an idiot...again! I swear, that girl just twists my head around."

"I'm on the outside looking in. My view is unimpaired by emotion."

"You do have a way of puttin' things," Caden remarked. "I'm still goin' into town to buy what I need. Even if she is gonna talk to me, my underwear and socks could be floatin' down the creek."

"Or in the manure pile," Richard laughed. "From everything you've told me, I wouldn't put it past her. Now I must get back to my desk. I assume Max mentioned we have Heather Chadwick arriving tomorrow."

"Yep, he couldn't wait to tell me."

"She has given us quite the list of requests, or rather, her mother has. I'm still organizing them all. I'd better get back to it."

"I don't know how you do it, Richard. I wouldn't have the patience to deal with these entitled, spoiled divas."

"Simple. I charge them a ton of money," Richard exclaimed.

"I'm ready to leave," Caden said grabbing his wallet. "I'll walk down with you."

"Lock your door," Richard said with a wink. "She might sneak up here and take something else."

"Such a brat," Caden mumbled.

"Maybe, but that's one of the things you love about her."

"I hate to admit it, but you're right Richard, you are so right."

DOWN IN THE PADDOCK, Bridget had stopped running with Valentino and was catching her breath. Panting and laughing, she watched the big gelding walk towards her.

"You are the best, most handsome fellow in the world," she said as he stopped in front of her. "Who are you? Where did Caden find you? I should make up with him just so I can spend time with you. I wish I could afford a horse like you. Maybe by the end of the summer I'll have earned enough working here to make that happen."

As if understanding her, he dropped his head over her shoulder and pulled her into his chest. There was little that touched Bridget more than a horse offering its affection and trust, and as her heart swelled, she could feel the heat at the back of her throat.

"Valentino, I can understand why that's your name. I'd call you that myself if you were mine. Can you keep a secret? I did something very naughty, and now I'm wondering if it was a mistake. I guess I'll find out soon enough."

The horse lifted his head and backed up, and sensing someone behind her, she turned around and saw Max walking towards them.

"You've really clicked with him," Max remarked as he approached.

"I have. He's a dream."

"You know you're gonna get to ride him, right?"

"I didn't know that for sure. Richard mentioned I could ask the trainer," she said, wishing the trainer was anyone but Caden. "I saw him in the dining room and he didn't say anything, but I hope I can. It's been love at first sight."

"No kiddin'," Max remarked. "Look at him, he's totally taken with you."

"I feel so honored," Bridget said stroking the horse's neck.

The sound of a car pulling into the stable yard caught their attention, and turning around she saw a silver Mercedes roll to a stop.

"Who's that?" Bridget asked.

"Richard," Max replied, but as he started to walk away to meet his boss, he stopped. "Nope, sorry, it's Caden Price, the trainer, drivin' Richard's car."

Bridget caught her breath, and as she watched Caden head towards the gate to enter the pasture, the butterflies in her stomach burst to life. He was wearing a change of clothes. That meant he'd unpacked his bag and knew what she'd done. But he was smiling, and she suddenly felt like jumping on the horse and galloping away.

"Hey, Caden. Have you seen this happy couple?" Max asked as Caden neared.

"I have. Valentino is crazy about you, Bridget."

"He's a special horse," she replied trying to control her nerves as she looked into Caden's hauntingly infinite blue eyes.

"Max, do you mind if I have a private word with Bridget for a minute?"

"No, no, be my guest. I have to get back to the barn anyway. When you're done, Bridget, could you please check in with me. I have some other details to go over with you."

"Yes, sure, of course," she replied wishing Caden hadn't found her.

They watched in silence as Max strode through the field and out the gate, then Caden began moving his hand across Valentino's back.

"I know what you did," he said, calmly. turning his eyes back to Bridget.

"What I did?" Bridget quipped raising her eyebrows. "What might that be?"

"Are they in the manure pile or the creek, or maybe," he paused, "under your pillow?"

"In your fucking dreams," she hissed.

"Ah, so you admit it then, and there's that word again," he said shaking his finger at her.

"I told you to stay out of my way."

"Actions, dear Bridget, you know what they say."

"What do they say?"

"Think about it," he said smiling down at her.

"Why are you here? Whatever it is you have to say, just say it and leave," she huffed. "Is it about riding this horse? Before you ask, yes, I would love to, and yes, I know that means I'll have to deal with you, and that's fine, I get it, and it'll be worth it. That's settled so now you can leave."

"Bridget, I've walked into this paddock and am standin' here for one reason, and one reason only, and it's not about ridin' Valento, though you can. No problem."

"What reason might that be?" she asked impatiently.

"I'm here to put you on notice."

"What do you mean, put me on notice?"

"Before this day is over, I'm gonna put you over my knee and spank you."

A hot, uninvited flush burned across Bridget's face, and a wave of something she couldn't identify surged through her body and landed between her legs. She wanted to snap back at him, say something funny and toxic, but not only was her mind a complete blank, her mouth had fallen utterly dry, and she was incapable of speech.

"My goodness, nothin' to say?" he quipped. "That's a first. I know I threatened it when we were together, but to quote an overused phrase, this is not a threat, it's a promise. I'll be seein' you at lunch, and then you'll ride Valentino, and then, at some point before midnight, you'll be over my knee gettin' your ass spanked. I should've done it a long time ago. Maybe we wouldn't be in this mess if I had. Still, better late than never."

Paralyzed, her face blazing, she watched him turn and stride away. Would he dare put her over his knee?

"Valentino, I shouldn't have raided his bag," she muttered anxiously. "What have I done?"

As if reading her mind, the horse snorted and shook his head.

"I'll just make myself scarce," she muttered finally finding her voice. "I'll have a wonderful ride on you, then disappear. I'll scout out a place he won't be able to find me. There are those woods behind the barn. I'll check them out before lunch."

But even as she mumbled the words, she knew wherever she tried to hide, he'd find her. She'd crossed some invisible line. She could feel it, and as she hugged the big, chestnut gelding, a warm shiver rattled down her spine.

CHAPTER FIVE

ENTERING THE DINING room a few minutes before midday, Bridget lingered, waiting to see where everyone would sit. When Caden chose to be next to Richard, she grabbed a chair at the other end of the table. Throughout the meal she studiously avoided eye contact, and when Richard introduced her, singing her praises and talking about what a first class horsewoman she was, she could feel Caden watching her. After his threat she was sure she'd fall victim to a blush if their eyes met, and she couldn't bear the thought.

But Caden had his own thoughts about why she'd been avoiding his gaze. He guessed she knew he was serious, and he wasn't about to beg forgiveness for a crime he didn't commit. Taking his clothes had been childish, but he wondered if she'd pulled the stunt to provoke him. Did she want him to take her in hand? Regardless, he was determined she'd be over his knee before the day was over.

As the lunch broke up, and the staff began going their separate ways, seeing her attempting a quick exit, Caden walked quickly across the room. Unfortunately for Bridget, several others were also heading towards the front door, and loitering in the hallway they had prevented her escape. Catching up to her, he grabbed her elbow and bustled her back into the dining room.

"I have to get to the barn," she protested trying to wrestle her arm from his firm grip.

"Bridget, you're behavin' like a child," he scolded. "You're embarrassin' yourself. This is important. Listen to me!"

Glancing around she spotted a few stragglers watching her, and though she stopped struggling she still didn't look at him, staring past him out the windows.

"I know we settled the fact that you're gonna ride Valentino, but Richard wants to watch. He and I will be at the stable at two o'clock. Max has put my saddle and bridal in the tack room, so he knows where it is. I'll expect you to be ready when we arrive. Don't get on him, just be ready and waitin.'"

"Fine," she muttered.

"Bridget, drop the attitude. I don't think you want Richard to see what a diva you can be," then lowering his voice and placing it at her ear, he added, "and it will only make me spank you harder."

Though she felt her face flame red and her stomach churn, she summoned the courage to lift her eyes.

"You, Caden Price, better not dare lay a hand on me. If you do, you'll be sorry."

She had hissed the words, and turning on her heel she stormed away.

As Caden watched her dramatic exit, he leaned his shoulder against the wall and crossed his arms. She was behaving exactly as he'd expected, and he couldn't be happier. Her protests were showing him how much she still cared.

Deciding to take the short nap he'd missed that morning, he trotted up the stairs to his room. Kicking off his boots and pulling off his jeans, he laid on the bed and sank into the inviting mattress, his tired body grateful for the respite, and closing his eyes he let out a long breath, allowing his mind to wander.

"Bridget, I don't know where I'm gonna catch you," he murmured, "but I can't wait to see your naked backside again. Yep, darlin', I'm gonna bare your butt and whip your bottom. You'll yell and holler and kick, but I'll keep on spankin' that ass until you promise to sit quietly and listen."

He felt his cock stir, and choosing to imagine the scene taking place in the small forest behind the barn, he pictured himself grabbing her wrists and pulling her towards a fallen tree trunk. Sitting on the rough wood, he yanked her over his lap and started smacking her perfectly lovely behind.

Pushing off his underwear, he clutched his cock and began to rub, but the image changed to one of his favorite times with her. It had happened inside the barn at his in-town facility, hidden behind stacks of hay bales.

He'd taken a brand new horse blanket and thrown it over the soft layers of scattered straw, then grabbing her, he'd kissed her fervently, and together they'd tumbled on top of it, urgently removing each other's clothes as their fever took hold.

As the memory raced through his head, he recalled the intense craving they'd had for one another, the soft whispers of love they had shared, and the promises they'd made. He ached to have her back in his arms, to knead her fleshy breasts and taste her pink, sweet kiss, and as the orgasm rippled through him, shooting his cream across his hand, though his deep groans signaled his release, they also spoke of his longing.

He laid still, letting the moment pass, then used the little energy he had left to roll over and grab some tissues.

"I'm gonna get you back if it's the last thing I do," he muttered as he wiped himself. "You've been missin' me as much as I've been missin' you. It doesn't matter how far you go, you can't escape your feelin's, and I think you're findin' that out."

AS CADEN WAS DRIFTING into a light doze, down at the barn, Bridget was in a silent, covert battle. Caden was in her head and refusing to leave. The feel of his fingers locked around her arm after lunch had sent a wet fire through her sex, and when he'd brought his lips to her ear, her heart had pumped so hard she thought it was going to burst from her chest.

Standing in the barn office, Max was holding a map and explaining how she could find her way to the nearby swimming hole, and though she was staring at the piece of paper in front of her, all she could see was Caden.

"There is the swimmin' pool area of course, you've seen that I assume?" Max asked.

"Yes, it's gorgeous," she nodded. "I love how it's decorated like a tropical island."

"Our female visitors prefer it, but a few of our male guests like to be a bit more adventurous. The swimmin' hole is as safe as any, but we still don't like anyone to be there by themselves. Since they have to walk past the barn to get there, we keep an eye out. If anyone ventures down there alone we don't stop 'em, we alert the house and someone zips down there."

"What if they don't want company?"

"It's written in the information that's sent out when they make their reservation, that everyone must be accompanied when going to the swimmin' hole. It's just the way it has to be."

"I see."

"If you notice anyone amblin' by and they start headin' down that path, you let me know, or if I'm not here, call Celeste right away."

"Got it," she nodded.

"You've got about an hour before Caden and Richard get here. Why don't you head on down there now. You need to know how to get there, and you also have to be familiar with it so if anyone asks, you can describe it. You've got your pager?"

"Yep, right here," she said pulling it from her pocket.

"You run into trouble, page me. I'm not goin' anywhere."

"What kind of trouble?"

"The kind I was talkin' about before. You know, snakes, or you trip and twist your ankle, anything."

"Oh, right," she said, vaguely recalling him mentioning such things.

"You okay?" Max asked, seeing the faraway look in her eye.

"What? Yes, fine," Bridget said quickly. "Just trying to take it all in. There's so much to this place, so many things I have to remember."

"It will click once the guests start arrivin'," he assured her. "If in doubt, ask. The only stupid question is the one that isn't asked."

"Thanks, Max."

"You have plenty of time, so don't hurry. Enjoy the hike."

"I will. I'll be back soon."

She left his office, and as she walked outside and started along the trail that would take her through the wooded area then down a gentle slope to the swimming hole, his words loitered in her head.

The only stupid question is the one that isn't asked.

"Shit. Should I have listened to Caden and let him tell me about that girl?" she murmured. "I didn't even ask who she was, I didn't ask him anything. Is it possible I've been totally and completely wrong about him? But they were together. He was holding her, and everyone told me he was a player. This is impossible."

She'd been so deep in thought she hadn't been paying attention to where she was walking, and as she scanned her surroundings, she realized she was about to enter the woods. As she fell under the lush, green canopy she broke into a smile. The air was cool, and the sounds of the birds, and the rustling of the leaves under her feet, brought forth a heavy sigh. The trail was easy to follow, and staring at the well-worn path under her feet, she wondered how many celebrities had preceded her.

At lunch Richard had read through the list of guests they'd be hosting for the month, and she'd learned the lunch was customary. It was held the last day of the four day hiatus so he could gather his troops together for an informal meeting and give everyone the opportunity to raise any issues they might have. As he'd called out the names of the visitors that would be coming in, she'd recognized most of them, but the girl arriving the next day was the most impressive; Heather Chadwick.

She was tall, willowy, blond and gorgeous, and at twenty-two, one of the youngest Oscar-winners in history, but she was not only a star on the screen, she was a hugely successful singer. Her latest album had gone double-platinum, and three of the songs were at the top of the charts.

"Heather Chadwick. How can a girl be born so lucky?" Bridget asked herself. "She's been given so much. I'll bet the men here will be falling all over her. Huh, I wonder if that's why Caden is staying over. I bet he won't be able to take his eyes off her."

She was reaching the end of the trees, and as the grassy meadow came into view, she could easily imagine a horse leisurely grazing.

"I'd love to bring Valentino to this spot. If it goes well today, I'll ask Caden if I can ride him out here. I guess I'll have to be civil in front of Richard anyway. I may as well crack a smile. It'll be worth it if I can get a trail ride out of it."

Walking through the field, she followed the bank down and could see the river on either side of the swimming hole. It was obvious the warm weather lowered the water level creating the unique, natural swimming pool, and reaching the bottom of the gentle slope she discovered two picnic tables tucked away under the shade of several trees. Securely covered trash cans provided a safe depository for people's garbage, and following a narrow path, she came across a small green shed surrounded by bushes. Opening the door she saw hooks on the walls, and a wooden plank bench in the middle.

"A changing room. How great is this?" she muttered.

Returning to the picnic table, she sat down and sank into the serenity around her, then closing her eyes she focused on the subtle sounds of nature. Birds were singing, she heard the distant croaking of frogs, and the rustling of small creatures in the undergrowth.

She suddenly found herself wishing Caden was with her. She was still crazy about him, and there was no way around it. As the pain surfaced, large droplets began to spill from her eyes, and dropping her head in her hands, she sobbed out her frustration.

"How am I ever going to get over you? Am I going to walk around with this ache inside me for the rest of my life? How could you have done it? Did you ever love me, or was it all just a joke to you, a game? Why, why, why are you here?"

A fresh wave hit, and clutching her stomach she doubled-over as her salty rain continued to fall. She let it flow, then finally straightening her body she wiped her wet face with her arm.

"I've cried too many fucking tears over you Caden Price," she declared. "I'm not doing it again, but I am going to ask the questions I never did. Max was right about that. The only stupid question is the one that isn't asked. You may or may not tell me the truth, but I have to ask, and I will."

Rising from the picnic table, she had another wander around to make sure she hadn't missed anything, then started back, climbing up the slope to the meadow. Reaching the top she turned around for a last look before heading into the trees and back to the barn. The sun was shimmering off the still water, and she thought it one of the prettiest views she'd ever seen.

"This is a magical place. It has everything. The people who can afford to come here are very fortunate. I wonder why Caden never mentioned it. That's another question I want answered," she murmured, then turning around, feeling calmer than she had in weeks, she headed into the woods.

CHAPTER SIX

WHENEVER RICHARD NEEDED to be somewhere on the property, he'd take himself there in a golf cart, and when he and Caden rolled up to the barn, Bridget was standing beside Valentino talking to him softly and stroking his face. The handsome gelding was tacked up and ready to ride, and to Caden's surprise she welcomed them with a happy smile.

"Good Lord, Caden, you weren't kidding," Richard exclaimed. "That is one beautiful horse. I'm looking forward to watching you ride, Bridget."

"Thanks, Richard, and I'm excited about getting on this big guy."

"No time like the present," Caden said. "Let's walk him out to the ring and I'll give you a leg up."

"Sounds good," she sweetly replied.

Caden had expected her to rebuff him, to tell him she didn't need his help, and as she moved ahead of them, Richard fell beside Caden and shot him a grin.

"See, you've made some progress," he suggested under his breath.

"A smile, yep that's progress," Caden replied, "but I'm sure it's for your benefit," silently adding, *and if she thinks bein' nice will get her out of her spankin', she's very much mistaken!*

The ring was a short walk, and as she entered Richard stayed by the fence while Caden followed her in. Taking the reins in one hand at the withers, and standing by the saddle, she lifted her foot and waited for him to give her a boost. She felt her pulse quicken. The moment brought back dozens of memories. He'd helped her up so many times before. He used to plant a kiss on her cheek, or send a whisper to her ear, and as he approached she held her breath.

"Don't worry about Richard and me. Just have fun," he said softly.

She felt a warm shiver, and swallowed back the emotion that was threatening to swell back up.

"Thanks," she mumbled, then his hands were around her calf and he was hoisting her into the saddle.

She gently lowered herself on to Valentino's back, and with a soft squeeze of her legs she asked him to move forward. In a few minutes she'd progressed into an easy trot, then a lope, and having gained her confidence she pushed him into a gallop. Watching from the fence, it was obvious to Caden the horse loved her, and the immediate comfort between horse and rider was remarkable.

Slowing to a walk, she decided to try some advanced moves, and found the horse more than up to the task, performing roll backs and quick stops like a champion. Trotting back to the fence, her face beaming, she saw Max had joined Caden and Richard.

"He is unbelievable," she declared. "A dream."

"You looked fantastic," Richard said admiringly. "How would you feel about giving our guests a demonstration some time."

"I'd be happy to, but I thought he was leaving?"

"Nothin"s been decided yet," Caden said thoughtfully, "and you did look terrific, Bridget. You two looked like you've been together for years. It's amazin' how you've gelled."

"I gotta say," Max chimed in, "I haven't seen ridin' like that in a while."

"He's so finely tuned," Bridget remarked petting his neck. "Not for a beginner. They'd be lost on him, and he'd get very confused."

"He's not for our guests, so no problem there," Richard assured her.

"I find him super responsive, but I haven't done any of what you just did. You're right, he shouldn't have a novice on his back," Caden agreed.

"Thanks so much for letting me ride him, Caden. It was great. Would it be all right for me to take him for a walk through the woods behind the barn?"

"Sure, he'd love that. Don't go down the slope to the water hole though, just to the edge of the meadow. I wouldn't trust that bank on horseback."

"Okay, no problem. Thanks."

Max had already started back to the barn, and as Caden watched her ride away, he couldn't help but feel her attitude had been sincere.

"I don't think her pleasant mood had anything to do with me," Richard said as if reading his mind.

"I was just thinkin' the same thing," Caden frowned. "How could she have done a one-eighty like that?"

"Maybe we're wrong. Maybe she's just a good actress. Look, she's getting off."

"Huh, that's weird. I'd better make sure there's no problem."

"I'm heading back to the house," Richard said walking towards the golf cart. "I still have things to get finished before tomorrow."

"Okay, Richard, I'll see you later."

Seeing Bridget lead Valentino into the barn, Caden broke into a jog, and catching up to them he found Bridget bent over looking at the horse's foot. As concerned as he was, he couldn't help but admire the view of her bottom so lusciously presented.

"What's the problem?"

"Loose shoe," she sighed standing up. "I heard the tink sound."

"Ah, the dreaded tink. I have some tools in the van. I'll take care of it."

"You do? That's great."

"Put on his halter and take him to the cross ties. I'll be right back."

"Will do," she replied.

Shaking his head, he chuckled as he left the barn and headed to his van.

"Yep, she does, she thinks she's gonna get outta that ass whippin'," he mumbled. "She's a smart girl. I've gotta give her credit for tryin'. Sure is nice though, to have her act like the girl I used to know."

Reaching his van he gathered up his tools and carried them back to the stable, but walking in he saw Valentino in the cross ties with Max watching him, and Bridget nowhere in sight.

"Where did she go?" Caden asked moving forward.

"I'm not sure," Max replied. "She poked her head in my office and asked me if I'd keep my eye on him until you got back."

"Huh. Maybe she got paged and had to go up to the house."

"I don't think so," Max said as he watched Caden pick up the horse's foot. "I could be wrong, but I thought I saw her headin' down the trail towards the swimmin' hole."

"Ah, thanks."

Valentino stood like a perfect gentleman as Caden pulled out the loose nail and tapped in a new one, but as he put the horse's foot down and dropped his tools into the carry box, he let out a grunt.

"What is it?" Max asked.

"He needs a farrier. I wanted to get him shod before I came up here but it didn't happen. My guy got sick. Do you have anyone comin' here anytime soon?"

"Nope, but we can call Butch in."

"Let's do that. I like Butch. I'm gonna chase up Bridget. Would you mind makin' that call?"

"I'll pick up the phone right now," Max promised, "and I'll put him back in his paddock. Bridget's a helluva rider. Glad to have her here. Seems like you two know each other. Don't mean to pry, but...?"

"Yeah, we know each other," Caden nodded. "I think I'll just leave it at that."

"I thought you might," Max grinned. "Leave the tools. I'll have them taken back to the van. You go chase that girl."

"Thanks, Max."

Walking quickly through the barn he started down the trail, and as he entered the woods he broke into a jog. He loved the smell and the coolness of the air, and as he approached the meadow he continued running until he reached the edge. Staring down the bank he saw Bridget sitting on the grass throwing stones into the pond, and glancing around he spied no other signs of life. Knowing exactly what he was going to do and where he was going to do it, he moved quietly down the gentle slope and stood behind her.

"Tryin' to hide from me, Bridget?"

Jumping to her feet she spun around, then took a few steps backwards.

"You scared me," she said angrily. "You shouldn't creep up on people like that."

"Bridget," he began, moving forward, "you and I are gonna have a serious talk," and suddenly, before she could speak or react, he was scooping her up and throwing her over his shoulder.

"What the hell? Put me down" she demanded pounding her fists into his back. "Put me down right now!"

"I will in a minute," he replied as he walked towards the small changing shed she'd found just a short time before, "but you'd better stop your squawkin.'"

"I won't, put me down," she yelled, kicking her legs as hard as she could.

The hard, shocking slap that hit her backside made her gasp, but it stopped her protests.

"One good swat and you're already listenin.' Maybe this won't take too long after all."

"You're a beast and a bully," she wailed.

"Maybe, but you're stubbon and a brat, so perhaps that evens things out."

He'd reached the shed, and opening the door he set her on her feet and sent her inside with another sound smack.

"Stop doing that," she hissed, twirling around to face him.

"I told you I was gonna spank you, and I am, and that's just the way it's gonna be."

"Don't you dare," she growled shaking her finger at him.

His hand shot out, grabbing her wrist, and before she could blink he had dropped on to the narrow wooden bench, yanked her over his lap, and placed his large leg over the back of hers.

"STOP!"

Her objection was met with another hot slap.

"If you keep this up, all this yellin' and carryin' on, I'll spank you real hard, you hear? So hard you'll be eatin' your dinner standin' up."

"Why are you doing this?" she bleated.

"It's real simple, darlin'. First, 'cos you're a brat and you need it. Like I said, if I'd done this sooner I think we could've avoided all the crap. Second, because you pulled that childish prank and snatched my underwear and socks. You think I'm gonna let you get away with that?"

"Apparently not," she sniped.

"Damn, girl," he retorted landing his hand.

"OW."

"Third, and most important, you've been completely unreasonable. You never let me explain you what you saw. You just jumped to conclusions, and I'm gonna spank you until you agree to sit quietly and listen to me."

"I will," she said quickly. "I've already decided to do that. I want to know, I do, I swear."

"You think sayin' that is gonna stop me from warmin' your ass?"

"Uh, maybe, maybe not, but it's the truth."

"Then I'm glad you finally came to your senses," he said, smoothing his hand over her bottom, "but it doesn't change how you acted back then, it doesn't mean you don't need a good spankin' for bein' such a brat, and it doesn't mean I'm not gonna swat you good for your prank, startin' right now!"

Raising his hand he let it fly in a flurry of slaps, delivering three at a time to each cheek, continuing until her entreaties and apologies started to sound sincere.

"Stand up and drop your jeans," he commanded moving his leg off hers.

"What? Are you serious?"

"Do I sound like I'm in a jokin' mood?" he said sternly, landing another hard smack. "If you don't do as I say I'll fetch me a switch."

"Okay," she said quickly, crawling off his lap, "but my ass is on fire already, and I said I was sorry."

"You're not sorry enough, not by a long shot," he retorted as he watched her unzip her pants and lower them to her knees. "Come on, back over my lap."

Leaning forward she wriggled into position, and ignoring her objections as he slipped her pink panties down to her thighs, he stared at her red backside and let out a sigh of satisfaction.

"I don't know what's gonna happen after we leave here, but before I finish reddenin' your backside, there's a couple of things I'm gonna say. Are you payin' attention?"

"Yes, I'm listening."

"I love you, Bridget, and back when I first said those words I meant them. I made you a promise, I told it was just you 'n me. What you saw was totally innocent, but instead of talkin' to me, instead of trustin' me, you believed all the bullshit. You think you were hurt? Damn, girl, you ripped my heart out."

"I'm sorry," she sighed. "You're right, I should have talked to you, asked you about it."

"Yeah, you're darn tootin' you should've. Now I've got a newsflash for you. I'm the reason you got this job. I arranged this whole thing."

"What? What are you talking about?"

"That's how much I care, girl, that's how much I needed to see you. You wouldn't even pick up the damn phone, and I was determined to find a way to get through to that stubborn, thick, obstinate head of yours. Now you're exactly where you deserve to be, over my knee gettin' your butt tanned."

Before she had a chance to respond he dispatched his hand, peppering her skin with a volley of swats, roaming the smacks from her sensitive sit spot to the center of her cheeks. He didn't pause, he didn't pay attention to her pleas and apologies, but continued to spank her until her pale moons had been transformed into a glowing pair of twin red planets.

"There. I hope I made my point."

"Ow! Ow! Caden, you spanked me so hard. It hurts so much."

"Good. I'm gonna rub you for a while and I want you thinkin' about everythin' I said. You hear me?"

"I do, Caden," she bleated. "I hear you."

He squeezed and fondled her scorched cheeks until he felt her begin to relax, then helping her up he brought her into his lap.

"Do you want me to hold you?"

"Very much," she managed. "I feel like I want to cry."

"Please, do, darlin'," he said tenderly as he helped her curl into his lap. "You need to, you need to cry in my arms, 'cos you've been cryin' without them and that's a real lonely feelin'."

"I'm such an idiot," she muttered as the first tears began to spill.

"No argument there," he sighed stroking her hair, "but I think you've learned a real valuable lesson."

"Many lessons," she sobbed, "and I'm so, so sorry I hurt you. That's the worst thing of all, that I hurt you. I can't believe you went to so much trouble to fix all this."

"When a cowboy loves a woman..."

"You said that to me so many times. You yelled at my door, and I've wondered almost every day how that sentence ends, but now I think I know," she sighed. "When a cowboy loves a woman he'll do anything for her. Caden, thank you, I've missed you so much."

"I've missed you too, darlin'. Been as mad as hell, but yeah, baby, I've missed you like crazy," he declared holding her tightly, "and that's not the end of that sentence, but it's close. You'll figure it out one of these days."

"Can't you just tell me?"

"Nope. You've gotta get there on your own."

"Ooh, my ass is so sore."

"I hope it stays that way for a while."

"Why?"

"It'll remind you how much I love you, and make damn sure you never pull crap like that again. You gotta problem, you face it, talk about it, and fix it. All you did was throw a huge hissy fit."

"What happens now?" she asked snuggling against him.

"We're goin' back to either your cabin or my room, and we're gonna talk."

"Your room please. There are too many staff members running around the cabins."

"My room it is."

"Caden, you're right about one thing."

"I'm right about a lot more than just one, darlin'."

"Probably," she mumbled.

"Go on, what's the one thing?"

"If you had, uh...never mind."

"If I'd spanked you ages ago, you wouldn't have been so quick to judge, and definitely would not have been so difficult."

"Yes," she whispered.

"I promise you," he said clutching her hair and pulling back her head. "If we find our way back together, you'd better believe I won't hesitate to take you in hand. I will blister your butt when you need it, so you'd better think about that, 'cos I mean it, sweetheart."

His words sent a rush of hot longing through her body, and she wriggled on his lap.

"Oh, Bridget," he sighed locking her eyes. "That's exactly what you want, isn't it, darlin'?"

"Yes, Caden, I didn't know that until just now, but yes, it is."

CHAPTER SEVEN

WHEN THEY REACHED HIS room, Bridget pulled off her boots and peeled off her jeans while Caden called Richard to let him know she'd be unavailable for the rest of the afternoon.

"Does this mean I've lost my latest employee?" Richard asked.

"I guess that's up to her, but I owe you one. A big one!"

"It didn't take you very long," Richard remarked. "I thought I'd be stuck with you for at least a week."

"No, thank the Lord," Caden replied. "We'll see you at dinner. I guess it's the last one with your troops until next month."

"Yes, but there won't be many there tonight. Most of the staff settle back into their cabin life the night before we start back up, and those that go home for a break rarely stop in at the house."

"You can count on us," he promised. "I'll see you soon."

Hanging up the phone he turned his attention to Bridget, engulfing her in his arms, and closing his eyes he smelled the familiar scent of her hair, a smell he'd been thinking about every day since their separation so many weeks before.

"Bratty Bridget, that's what you were, and such a stubborn girl."

"I know, I'm sorry. I could say it a hundred times and it wouldn't be enough."

"Once is all I need, if you mean it," he said softly.

"I do," she sighed, "you know I do. I hope you don't mind me pulling off my jeans. They were scratching my skin."

"Takin' off your jeans is something I'll never complain about," he said with a smile. "Let's sit on the bed, it'll be a bit more comfortable for your butt than the couch. It's time to straighten all this out."

"I still can't believe you got me this job," she declared as they walked slowly to the bed. "It's such an exclusive place. Why didn't you ever tell me about it?"

"First things first," he said firmly. "What you saw."

"Right," she nodded.

Climbing on to the bed, she sat next to him, sitting propped up against the headboard with her arm looped around his.

"That girl you saw me hugging," Caden began, "her name is Melinda Goodwin. Valentino was her horse and-"

"What? Valentino?" she interrupted. "I don't understand."

"Let me finish and you will," he scolded.

"Sorry. It just took me by surprise."

"I found Melinda that horse about six years ago. She grew up with him, competed, did real well, but she was headin' off to college overseas and she couldn't bear to sell him to strangers, so she asked me if I'd give him a home. She knew I'd take good care of him, and she'd be able to visit him whenever she wanted. Obviously I can't do that with every horse I sell, but he's a special one, and I've always been real fond of Melinda, so I agreed. That hug you saw was because she'd just said goodbye to him. She needed to see me, get some comfort and reassurance."

"Ooh, no. Caden, I'm so, so sorry."

"Why wouldn't you talk to me?" he asked, a deep frown crossing his brow.

"I don't know. I should have. I guess it was because when I first starting going out with you, everyone told me I was crazy, that you were a player, that you were a cheat."

"Hey! You can stop right there. I've never been a cheat. Yeah, I dated a lot, and some of the girls I went out with thought there was more to it than there was, but I never lied to any of 'em. Not one."

"I'm so embarrassed."

"You ever hear the sayin', a girl's gotta kiss a lotta frogs before she finds her handsome Prince?"

"Of course."

"Well, darlin', it goes the other way too. A guy's gotta kiss a lotta girls before he finds his Princess."

"I guess that's true."

"I thought I'd found her," he murmured staring into her eyes. "Was I wrong?"

"No! No, you weren't, you aren't, please don't think that."

"You've gotta trust me. If you don't trust me, Bridget, we've got nothin'."

"I do, I will. Can you forgive me?"

"Sure, but as far as gettin' back together, you've gotta know in your heart that I'm a good guy, you've gotta really believe it. Can you do that?"

"Yes, I can, I do, and if I freak out about something I promise I'll tell you."

Abruptly moving, he put his hands around her waist and slid her down the bed, then climbing over her, he grabbed her wrists and pinned them on either side of her head.

"It's okay if you get a bit jealous or insecure, we all do sometimes," he said, his voice low and deep, "but if you act out, or fly off the handle at me, I'm gonna tan your backside, you hear me?"

"Yes," she whispered.

His determined blue eyes were boring into hers, but they began to soften, a smile slipped across his lips, and he slowly lowered his head. Bridget closed her eyes, aching for his kiss.

Answering her prayer, with a feather touch he whispered his lips across hers, then began to press with an urgent fervor, devouring her mouth, making her body tingle and fueling her burning need.

"Caden," she breathed as he broke away, "I've missed you so much."

"I can feel it," he purred moving his lips to her neck. "You're starvin', aren't you, darlin'?"

"Yes, so starving."

"Tell me the truth, have you been with anyone since me?"

"No, no I couldn't even think of it."

"Neither have I," he smiled. "I was tempted a few times, but I couldn't. Good, then I don't have to mess with a condom."

"No, you don't, and I never went off the pill," she murmured, lifting her chest, pressing her breasts against him.

"Take off the rest of your clothes," he growled slipping from the bed.

Stripping off, he watched her pull her T-shirt over her head, and when she slid off her panties and unhooked her bra, her glorious nakedness sent his cock surging to life. Falling back on the bed he placed his hands around her fleshy mounds, holding them tightly, and dropping his lips to her nipples he sucked and tongued, eliciting gasps and soulful moans as her fingers dug into his back.

"Caden, take me, please, take me."

Lifting his head he met her eyes, then slipping a hand between her nether lips he let out a low groan.

"Darlin', you're soppin'."

"I know," she gasped, "I need you, please."

Pushing her legs apart he kneeled up between them, and grabbing her hips, clutching tightly, he jerked her into his pelvis.

"You said you want me to take you. Let's double-check," he teased, fingering her soaked, hungry channel.

"Please," she begged.

Placing his cock at her entrance, he plunged forward, then holding her still he began to stroke, her cries and gasps feeding his lust. When her eyes closed and her back arched, he paused, slowly withdrew, and flipped her over.

"Elbows and knees," he directed.

She moaned loudly as she assumed the lewd position, and as his hands began moving across her scarlet moons, then grasped them, she buried her head in the down comforter and let out a cry.

"You want my cock again?"

"Yes, yes, please."

"Yes, please, Sir," he said sternly.

"Sir?"

"You heard me. Things are gonna be different this time around. You want my cock back inside you?"

"Yes, please, Sir," she wailed.

Lining himself up, he paused a moment, then charged himself home, drawing a muffled howl.

"Now I'm gonna ravage you," he declared, "and I'm gonna do somethin' else, somethin' you resisted. This time, though, you're gonna mind. You understand?"

"Yes, Sir," she groaned knowing exactly what he meant.

Bridget was overcome. This was a different Caden. This Caden wasn't going to tolerate any of her nonsense or let her throw tantrums, and as he continued fondling her tender backside, she realized he would no longer allow her to dictate what they did in bed. A shard of panic sizzled through her, but it was panic tinged with excitement.

"You like me takin' charge like this, don't you, darlin'? The truth."

"I do," she bleated, "I love it. I love it."

"I'm still gonna love you and protect you and be real sweet, but you're gonna get to know the other side of Caden Price. It started with that spankin', and now it's gonna continue. You know what I mean?"

"Yes, Sir, I think I do."

"Are you gonna give me any trouble?" he asked landing a hard swat in the center of her backside.

"Ow! No, Sir."

His cock was buried in her depths, and as he began to pump with slow, forceful strokes, he placed the tip of his finger against her dark back hole.

"Ooh, Sir."

"Behave," he warned, "don't you dare pull away."

Gritting her teeth, Bridget turned her crimson face into a pillow. His cock was divine, but the finger wanting access to her forbidden back door was almost more than she could bear.

"That's my girl, just a little bit this first time, but I'm gonna train you, darlin', and you're gonna learn to love it."

In spite of his dire promise, she could feel her climax hovering, and she moved a hand between her legs.

"What are you doin'? You wanna play with yourself, you've gotta ask."

"I do?" she muttered, wishing the finger between her cheeks would stop touching her.

"Oh, yeah, your pussy is mine now. I told you, things are gonna be different. You don't get to touch it whenever you want. Only I have that right."

A fresh surge of heat washed through her, and in spite of the lecherous finger, she bucked back, inadvertently causing it to slip inside.

"Sir," she begged, "may I touch myself?"

"Yeah, darlin', make yourself come for me right now."

Gratefully moaning into the pillow, she brought her hand to her magic button and began to rub. Her moment was over her, threatening to break, and as she urgently massaged her clit, his strokes accelerated, and his dreaded finger continued to press forward. The climactic bubble was huge, as immense as a hot air balloon. She could feel it threatening to break, and she held her breath, then suddenly erupting she toppled through the mighty orgasm in a crescendo of convulsions.

Watching her climax sent Caden into a powerful release, and he groaned loudly as he surrendered to a multitude of spasms. The weeks of waiting were culminating in an explosion that made him squeeze his eyes shut and clench his teeth. When the last pulsing moment passed, and his shriveled cock fell away, he glanced down at her limp body. She was panting, deep in her bliss, and staggering from the bed into the bathroom he washed up, then returned with a clean, dry face cloth.

"Hey," he purred stretching out next to her and placing the cloth between her legs.

"Caden," she breathed opening her eyes.

"Come here, darlin,'"

Rolling into his arms, sighing a heavy sigh, she let herself drift, and when she began to open her eyes she was filled with gratitude, completely amazed by what he'd done to reunite them.

"Back on the planet?" he purred.

"I am," she smiled shifting back and staring up at him. "I still can't believe what you did to bring us back together."

"I had to," he said simply, "and I never told you about this place because I was savin' it for a surprise. You know I wanted to bring you to my ranch, but you were always too busy."

"I remember," she nodded, "but I didn't realize it was in this area. I thought it was north, not south."

"Just as well," he remarked. "Anyway, I was gonna have us spend a couple of nights there, then drive down here for a romantic getaway. Richard was gonna squeeze me in when he had a vacancy. He's almost always booked out."

"Oh, Caden."

"I didn't wanna spoil the surprise."

"Can we stay here now? Wait, what am I saying? Do I have a job, or was that just-"

"You most definitely have a job," he interrupted. "Richard is always lookin' for good people, especially this time of year, but he knew there was a chance you'd leave if we got back together. If you wanna stay and work, it's up to you."

"It's up to us," she said softly. "I do love it here, and I think it would be a fun job for a while, but I don't want to be away from you."

"My ranch is about an hour away drivin' the horse van, so about forty-five minutes in a car. I spend most of the spring and summer down here. My ranch is also a breedin' farm, and we have a lotta babies. I oversee all that."

"Really?"

"You can come and spend your days off with me if you want, and I can visit you here."

"As long as I can still see you, I'll stick around."

"Don't tell Richard you're stayin' unless you're sure."

"I love this place, and what he wants me to do here is right up my alley. Teach people how to ride, take them out on the trails, all that stuff. I need to get to know the horses though. Max has told me about them, but I need to spend a day just riding them all, learning their habits."

"They've all be trained by me, so you shouldn't have too much trouble," he smiled.

"Caden, this, uh, other you," she said quietly.

"Uh-huh."

"Why didn't you let me see it before?"

"It's a timin' thing. Not every woman wants a man like me, and I don't like to show my hand, if you'll pardon the pun, until I'm sure the lady won't run screamin' from the room."

"You weren't sure about me?"

"You're a real headstrong girl, Bridget, and some headstrong girls are difficult because they're lookin' for a man to step up, but others, well, others are just that way. Opinionated, obstinate, and bratty, and they don't wanna change. I was fairly sure you'd respond like you have, and I was close to openin' the door, lettin' you have a peek, when everything blew up."

"Oh, I see," she murmured. "Sorry about that."

"You ever heard of domestic discipline?"

"Um, no. What's that?"

"When you come back to my place I want you to get on my computer and look it up, but it's exactly what it sounds like."

"Oh, I get it. You get to spank me when you think I need it. You're the man about the house."

"Yep. Are you all right with that?"

"Very all right," she sighed leaning into him.

"I'll keep that butt tender."

"I know you will, but you'll also take care of me, you'll take care of my heart."

"Yes, darlin', I will."

"I guess I should call Richard."

"You're not goin' anywhere. I wanna hold you for a little while longer."

"Yes, Sir," she smiled.

"There you go," he sighed, "now that works."

CHAPTER EIGHT

CELESTE, RICHARD AND three other staff members were the only people at the large table when Bridget and Caden entered the dining room for dinner.

"Ah, hello you two," Richard smiled. "I wasn't sure if we'd see you."

"I promised we'd be here," Caden replied. "You know I'm a man of my word."

"Yes, I do. Hello, Bridget. Tell me, am I losing you?"

"I'd love to stay on if you'd like me to."

"Will someone please tell me what's happening?" Celeste asked. "Why would you be leaving? You just got here."

"Uh, Bridget and I had a bit of a fallin' out," Caden said pulling out a chair for her then sitting down himself, "and she wouldn't talk to me, so Richard here, bein' the gallant guy that he is, offered her a job so I could corner her and try to work things out."

"How romantic! I wish a man would do something like for me," Celeste said wistfully.

"Maybe one day he will," Bridget offered. "It was kind of shocking though, shocking but wonderful."

"Hmm, speaking of shocking but wonderful, I suspect Heather Chadwick will be both of those things when she arrives tomorrow," Richard remarked. "Heather and her mother will be the only guests for a couple of days, and I'm sure she'll expect to be waited on hand and foot."

"What time will she get here?" Bridget asked.

"Late morning. There's a private airfield about twenty minutes away, that's where our guests land and we send a car to fetch them. Her flight's due in at ten-thirty. Her mother told me she's a horse nut, so I'm sure you can expect her at the barn at some point. Jane and Tim will be there tomorrow, so you won't have to deal with her by yourself. As I told you on the phone, those are the other two handlers. They're used to working with our celebrity guests. Jane is Max's right hand, so she's who you should go to first with any questions."

"I don't mean to interrupt, but I'm starvin'," Caden declared wanting to change the subject. *Jane. I totally forgot about her. I'm gonna have to deal with her before she runs into Bridget.*

"How can you bring up food when we're talking about meeting Heather Chadwick?" Bridget exclaimed.

"Simple, like I said, I'm starvin'," he replied, "and I'm not real impressed with most of the Hollywood gang. Narcissists, most of 'em."

"Well, I can't wait to meet her," Bridget declared.

"You have your choice of roast beef or salmon," Richard said answering Caden's question. "Here comes Julia now. I don't think anyone else will be joining us so we can place our orders."

"Thank goodness," Caden said gratefully.

"Richard, can you tell me about this place?" Bridget asked. "How did you end up here? It's so gorgeous."

"I'd been in the high-end hospitality business for years, and it dawned on me one day, that what these famous people really wanted was a true escape," Richard explained. "A place where they couldn't be hounded by photographers, and the general public simply didn't exist. Somewhere they could lounge by a pool, or ride a horse, play tennis, or sleep all day, but in a luxurious home-like atmosphere. It took me a couple of years to find this property, and it fit the bill."

"Was the private airfield here then?"

"That's what clinched it. There are some extremely wealthy ranchers in this county and it was built to service them."

"I wondered about that. I thought it was weird there'd be a place for private planes in an area that feels like it's in the middle of nowhere."

"That was the other thing. It does feel like the middle of nowhere, and it kind of is," Richard grinned.

"At last, here comes some food," Caden said as Julia arrived with two large salad bowls.

"I'll be bringing in some hot appetizers in a minute," she said placing the bowls on the table.

The meal continued in a light vein, Caden and Bridget's joy shedding its light across the table, and when the last dish was cleared, Caden suggested a walk through the grounds.

"Bridget, you should definitely go," Richard agreed. "All the lights are on tonight."

"Lights?"

"We have landscaping lights," Celeste explained. "They've been off for the last four days, but they're back on. It's like a fairyland out there."

"Oh, yes, I'd love to see it," Bridget said eagerly. "That was a fabulous dinner, Richard, thank you. I'm surprised so few of the others were here."

"You're welcome. I'm glad you two joined us. As far as the rest of the staff goes, the night before business starts back up they like to stay in their cabins."

"You ready?" Caden asked rising from his chair.

"I am," Bridget said taking his hand. "Take me where you will."

Holding hands they left the grand dining room and headed outside, and as they closed the front door, Bridget looked around and took a long deep breath.

"What a lovely night," she sighed. "Can we walk down to the barn? I'd like to check on Valentino, make sure he's happy in his paddock."

"I'm sure he is," Caden said putting his arm around her, "but I'd like to check on him too. Max was going to call the shoer. I'm not sure if I'll be able to see anything in the dark, but I'd like to take a look."

As they began their walk, the many lighting effects came into view, and she was completely captivated.

"Celeste was right," she said softly. "It is like a fairyland, and it's so romantic."

"You know what I'm thinkin'," he whispered.

"Exactly the same thing I am," she giggled. "Will the barn be empty?"

"Let's find out."

They were soon walking into the stable yard, and finding it quiet and serene, Caden twirled her around with one hand, then pulled her against him.

"Bridget," he breathed, "I'm gonna make love to you, but slow, real slow. I wanna explore you all over again."

"Yes, please," she sighed, and lifting her arms around his neck she brought her lips up to his.

She kissed him longingly, her mouth pressing sweetly, and when she slipped her tongue between his teeth he clutched a fistful of her hair, jerking her head back.

"I might have to take back that slow part," he said huskily, his blue eyes glinting into hers, "I want you so bad!"

Swooping her up he carried her into the barn. It was dark, but the outside lighting cast a subtle glow, and moving into the hay area he laid her down.

"I'll be right back," he promised. "I'm gonna go grab a blanket from my van."

The hay was kept at the back of the barn, and though it had a sliding door that was closed in inclement weather, being spring it was wide open. Gazing at the large silver orb hanging low in the black sky, she could hardly believe she was back with Caden.

"My God, I'm so lucky he didn't give up on me. How can I ever repay him for that?"

Deciding to surprise him, she quickly stripped off, and had just stretched out on top of her clothes when she heard him returning.

"What do we have here?" he said with a wide grin walking towards her.

"A naked lady waiting for you," she laughed.

He flapped open the blanket, and as she rolled on to it, he hurriedly undressed and dropped down next to her.

"You know," he said leaning over her, "I didn't have any dessert, and," he said with a wicked look as he retrieved a bandana from his pocket. "I seem to recall you likin' a blindfold."

"Oh, yes," she breathed, "I loved it when you did that."

Slipping it over her eyes he tied it securely behind her head, then pushing her back he began trailing his lips across her neck. He lingered, tasting her flesh, then journeyed his tongue across her shoulder to her breasts, lapping hungrily at her nipples before taking them into his mouth. Her soft moans echoed through the still night, and when he cruised his lips to her stomach, promising to head further south, she wriggled, aching for the tantalizing touch she knew was coming.

Though his cock was rigid and demanding attention, Caden was taking his time, relishing the taste and feel that was uniquely hers, but as he slipped between her legs to kiss her inner thighs, her plaintive begging sent a fresh surge of need to his loins.

"I'm gonna fuck you so hard," he grunted, gripping her hips and moving his mouth to her pussy.

Hearing the hushed comment, Bridget squirmed in his grasp, inciting his lust. Diving his tongue into the promised land he lapped salaciously, then swirled his tongue around her clit. She cried out her delight, and filled with a voracious fever, Caden attacked his job, devouring her with an all-consuming passion.

"I'm there," she panted, "please..."

Her fingers curled into the blanket as her gasps of pleasure announced her quick, powerful orgasm. Caden didn't let up, milking her moment until her cries became soft whimpers, then sliding up her body he drove his cock home.

Her pussy was drenched, his cock was ravenous, and laying on top of her he brought his hands underneath her bottom, clutching her tender cheeks as he stroked. Riding her relentlessly, his nostrils were filled with the heady smell of the barn mingled with the warm feminine fragrance radiating from his girl, and he could feel his eruption rising to the surface.

Grunting and groaning as his spasm rattled down his spine, he felt her stiffen below him. She was calling his name, and he realized she was in the throes of a second release. Pumping harder, her taut nipples rubbing against his chest, one last, intoxicating convulsion shot forth, and he was done. Rolling off her on to his side, his heart battering his chest, he took several long deep breaths.

"Caden, are you okay?" she breathed.

"If I was any more okay they'd have to lock me up," he panted. "You?"

"The same," she panted. "It was almost worth all the drama for this."

"Maybe, but I don't want a repeat, thanks very much."

"Me either," she sighed. "The moon is so full tonight. I feel like I could reach out and touch it. It's almost like it's there just for us."

"Maybe it's a perigree moon," he suggested.

"What's a perigree moon?"

"It's when the moon is the at the closest point to the earth."

"I'd like to buy a telescope," she snuggling closer to him. "I think it would be amazing to see all the craters and everything."

"I have one at my ranch."

"Really? Okay, now I'm excited. I'm not sure I can wait five days. I'm going to suggest to Richard that he get one for this place."

"That, my angel, is an excellent idea. Wait...did you just hear something?"

"Uh, no, I don't think so," she replied.

"Probably just a creature, but we should probably get dressed," he said kissing her warmly.

"Probably, but I hate to end this," she lamented. "It's so wonderful laying here with you."

"Let's wander over to the swimming pool. We can lounge there, maybe risk a skinny dip."

"You think we could?" she smiled.

"Let's find out," he winked.

Rising to their feet, Caden finished dressing first, and folded up the blanket.

"I'm going to run this back. I'll only be a minute."

She watched him march away, and pulling on her boots and T-shirt, she stuffed her bra into the pocket of her jeans. Still on a cloud she wandered into the barn, but to her shock, the lights came on, and she heard the sound of a horse's feet.

"Who the hell is bringing a horse in at this time of night," she muttered.

Hurrying forward she was shocked to see a tall, attractive blond girl placing Valentino in the cross ties.

"Uh, excuse me," Bridget called.

"Who are you?" the girl asked frowning at her.

"I'm Bridget Cooper. What are-?"

"Oh, of course, you're the new girl," the young woman said cutting her off. "I'm Janc, Max's assistant. Since you're here, would you go into the tack room and bring me out a grooming kit."

"I don't understand."

"You don't know what a grooming kit is?"

"Of course, but why, what are you doing with him?" Bridget asked pointing at Valentino.

"I'm going to clean him up, throw a sheet on him, and put him in a stall so he'll be ready for me to ride in the morning."

"No, no, no!"

"What?" Jane scowled.

"No, you can't ride him, no-one can ride him, only me."

"What the hell are you talking about?"

"And he doesn't need to be in a stall all night, and he sure as hell doesn't need a sheet. It won't drop below sixty tonight."

"Okay, listen, Bridget," Jane said tersely, "you don't have a say in-"

"No!" Bridget shouted interrupting her. "You listen. That horse belongs to—"

"Me!" Caden announced walking in on the squabble. "Bridget's right, Jane. He's not for public consumption, he shouldn't be in a stall in this barn all by himself overnight, and he sure as hell doesn't need a sheet on him."

"Caden," Jane said excitedly, and to Bridget's shock, the girl completely ignored Caden's lecture and walked quickly towards him. "I didn't expect to see you until tomorrow," she continued. "Are we finally going to pick up where we left off?"

Bridget watched, holding her breath, as the girl attempted to put her arms around his neck.

"No, Jane, absolutely not," he said firmly, grabbing her wrists and pushing her away. "Bridget is with me, I'm with Bridget, I mean, Bridget and I are together."

"Obviously you two need to talk," Bridget quipped grabbing a lead rope. "I'm taking Valentino back to his paddock."

"Wait, let me see his feet," Caden exclaimed.

Marching away from Jane he walked directly across to Bridget and Valentino, and as he leaned down to see if the horse had been shod, he glanced up at her.

"Nothing happened with Jane," he whispered. "I'll explain later."

"Looks as if the shoer did come," Bridget remarked trying to compose herself.

"Yes, he did, excellent. Let's take him out together."

"Are you sure? You don't need to, uh, finish your conversation with her?"

"Absolutely sure," he nodded standing up. "There's nothing to finish."

"Why did you bring that horse here if he's not for the guests?" Jane demanded as Caden and Bridget began leading Valentino from the barn.

"I have my reasons," Caden said briskly.

"Good to meet you, Bridget," Jane quipped. "When you get here in the morning you can start by cleaning the tack."

"Ignore her, she's baiting you," Caden said under his breath.

"It's not easy," Bridget whispered.

"Do it anyway. Deep breaths, count to ten."

By the time they'd reached the paddock Bridget was feeling better, and releasing Valentino into the field, she looped her arms around Caden's waist and leaned into his chest.

"I was so angry when I saw her with him, and when she started towards you, I wanted to rip her hair out," she muttered.

"I know. I could see the smoke coming out of your ears."

"What happened with her."

"Nothing, not really. We ended up in the barn late one night, got to talkin', she made it clear she wanted somethin' to happen, but I told her I had to get back to my ranch. She said we could pick up where we left off on my next visit. I didn't say anythin', but that's what she was referrin' to."

"It was that recent?"

"No, it was a while back, but she was always out on a trail ride or teachin' the few times I was here. We didn't even exchange words."

"Oh, I see," Bridget said softly. "The question remains though, how am I going to work with her now? This is going to be impossible."

"You want my advice?"

"Yes, definitely," she nodded.

"When you arrive in the morning, make nice. Apologize-"

"Apologize? You're kidding?"

"Nope, apologize, make friends, otherwise you're right, it will be impossible."

"Shit."

"I think we should go up to bed."

"I agree. I want a shower and a cuddle."

"Me too," he said giving her a squeeze.

"Will she listen, about Valentino, I mean?" she asked as they began walking.

"She should. Max knows, and Max is the boss."

"That's something, I guess."

Overcome by a heavy yawn, she rested her head on his shoulder as they made their way up the drive.

"A shower and sleep, that's what you need," he declared.

"What a divine thought, to sleep in your arms all night," she said with a sigh, quietly deciding she'd roll with the punches, but if the girl was a total bitch, Bridget made up her mind she'd quit.

CHAPTER NINE

BRIDGET WAS DUE AT the barn at eight o'clock, so Caden had set the alarm for seven. When it buzzed them awake, Bridget groaned her displeasure and rolled over to hold him.

"Don't let me leave," she mumbled.

"You have to get back to your cabin, shower, and have breakfast, you need to move your butt."

"Nope, I refuse," she said firmly, and reaching down she took hold of his semi-hard member.

"No fair," he grumbled closing his eyes.

"I know, but I'm not leaving this bed until I have my way with you," she muttered, continuing her salacious massage. "There," she whispered, feeling his cock harden in her fingers. "See how easy that was?"

Rolling on to her side, she reached behind her and guided him into her hungry canal, then letting out a long, soft moan she pushed back, impaling herself.

"Damn, girl, you are so willful," he mumbled as he held her hip and began to pump.

"That's not a complaint is it?" she murmured.

"Not right now," he grunted.

Moving his hands to her breasts he tweaked and rubbed, then dropping his lips to her neck he sucked in her skin.

"Oh, Caden, this is the only way to wake up."

"Mmm, I agree," he muttered.

Closing her eyes she sank into the joy of his slow, forceful thrusts, and when he moved his hand from her breasts to her clit, she caught her breath.

"Feel good?" he whispered.

"So good. If you keep doing that..."

"I know, darlin'. I'm not gonna stop. I'm gonna fuck you till you come, and when I get you back to my ranch, I'm gonna be doin' a whole lot more than that."

"You are?" she squeaked feeling her moment approach.

"Oh, yeah, I'm gonna start your trainin'."

"My training?" she breathed.

"I'm gonna dress your naked body in ropes, I'm gonna flog your ass, I'm gonna train your mouth, and you know what else, don't you?"

His promise sent her tumbling into her release, and as the spasms sent the tingling prickles through her limbs, she heard him groan through his moment as his essence spewed inside her.

"I'm sorry," she moaned, "I cannot leave this bed."

"I know," he said cuddling her, "and I don't want you to."

She felt herself drift away, lost in a sea of serenity, but his alarm clock buzzed a second time.

"I hate that sound. I remember that clock from before."

"Different clock."

"I still hate it," she grumbled.

"Darlin', you've gotta get up. It's almost seven-twenty."

"I can't stand it," she yawned, and reluctantly moving from his arms she stumbled from the bed and headed into his bathroom. "I'm going to shower here, then all I have to do is run back to the cabin and change clothes."

"You need to eat," he called after her.

"I will," she called back.

Lounging in the bed, he thought about what had happened the night before. He'd told Bridget the truth about Jane, but what he'd left out was that Jane had done more than subtly suggest they get together. She thrown herself at him, pulling off her shirt and grabbing his crotch as she'd tried to kiss him. Her aggression had been startling, and looking back on it he wondered if he'd been remiss in not reporting the incident to Richard. If she'd been that assertive with him, it was possible she might try the same thing with the celebrity guests.

Hearing the shower fall quiet, he turned his attention to the bathroom door, and when Bridget stepped in the room with a towel around her chest and her wet hair falling around her shoulders, he wanted to jump from the bed and ravage her all over again. As she reached for her clothes, he slipped from the bed and ambled across to her.

"Listen, my lovely, you need to make your peace with Jane."

"I know," she nodded, "and I will."

"I don't wanna hold anything back," he said carefully, "but I also don't wanna interfere with your success here, and for that to happen, you'll need to get along with her."

"What do you mean, hold anything back?" she asked feeling her heart jump. "Was there something between you two that you didn't tell me about last night?"

"No, absolutely not," he said firmly.

"Then what?"

"I'm only gonna tell you this so you have the whole truth, and then, no matter what she says, or anyone else says, you'll know it, okay?"

"Okay."

"Jane was very aggressive with me. She literally, physically, uh, came at me. I had to push her off."

"Really? Huh."

"I did though, push her off me. I barely saw her after that until last night. I had no interest in her, and that's it."

"Thanks, Caden. I'm not surprised," she said pulling on her T-shirt.

"You're not?"

"Not at all, she's the type. She's naturally pushy. It's her nature."

"Huh, yeah, I guess you're right," he nodded. "That's another reason I love you so much."

"Why?"

"Because you have an instinct about things, about people. You can read them."

"I didn't read things right when I saw you and Melinda," she sighed.

"That was different, you were emotional, you were hurtin', you just reacted, and you had people yappin' in your ear, but that's behind us now."

"Yes, sorry, you're right. I have to run. Will you meet me in my cabin for lunch at midday?"

"Of course I will," he said with a final hug. "Now, scoot."

He watched her hurry from the room, and was about to enter the bathroom when his phone rang. Returning to the bed he sat down and picked it up, wondering who would be calling him so early.

"Hello?"

"Good morning."

"Richard, what can I do for you this morning?"

"Max just called me. He's sick. He sounded terrible, coughing, sneezing."

"Oh, no."

"Obviously I don't want him around anyone, God Forbid we have a flu outbreak."

"God Forbid," Caden agreed.

"He said that Jane and Tim will be taking some of the horses out on the trail today, but he wants Bridget to ride the other horses in the arena so she can get to know them. The grooms are there, but with Max sick, and the guests arriving, I'd feel better if you were around the barn, you know, just to keep your eye on the place. Would you mind?"

"Not at all."

"I don't know when you have to get back to your ranch, but-"

"Richard, it's not a problem. If you have room for me, I'm happy to stick around until Max is feeling better. I have no desire to leave Bridget right now. I'm glad of the excuse to stay."

"We'll need your room in about three days, maybe it's four, you need to check with Celeste, but you can always stay with Bridget in her cabin when the time comes."

"I'm sure we'll be happy wherever we are," Caden replied.

"I appreciate it, Caden, thanks. After Heather Chadwick arrives I'm going to run into town and pick up some medication for Max. Do you need anything?"

"Nope, but if it's okay to leave the barn for an hour, I'd like to come with you. I wanna buy some flowers for Bridget, and I wanna pick them out myself."

"Leaving for an hour or so will be fine. It's more the general feeling that someone is at the helm."

"I get it. I'll head down there after breakfast."

Hanging up the phone, Caden padded into the bathroom and turned on the shower, and as he stepped under the water he felt a wave of relief.

IN HER CABIN EATING a bowl of granola, Bridget was deep in thought. She was grateful Caden had told her the whole story. Now she knew what kind of woman Jane was, and she had no doubt that Jane was going to be trouble with a capital T. She knew the type well. Women who saw the barn as their domain and did whatever was necessary to retain control and chase away anyone who posed a threat.

"She probably has Max wrapped around her little finger," Bridget muttered angrily. "She may be able to ride and teach, but she's not a horse person. A horse person wouldn't put a blanket on a horse on a warm night and make him stay in a stall just because it's easier. She's selfish and self obsessed, and I'll bet she's totally pissed that Caden is spoken for."

Leaving the granola half-eaten, she grabbed her pager, and heading out the door she hurried across to the barn. She didn't want to give Jane any excuse to rail at her. Reaching the stable yard a couple of minutes after eight, she walked into the barn and discovered it empty except for the grooms, but there was evidence that two horses had been in the cross ties.

"Shit. Valentino," she muttered, and running outside she glanced across at the paddock.

The big chestnut was happily swishing his tail and grazing on the lush green grass, and letting out a breath Bridget ambled back to the barn.

"Where's Max," she asked one of the workers.

"Sick. Jane said she left a note for you in the tack room."

"Okay, thanks, Jimmy."

Walking into the tack room she looked around, and saw sponges, rags and cleaning products on top of a trunk, along with a note.

Clean all the tack before lunchtime. The first guest arrives today and it has to be ready.

Bridget burst out laughing.

"What's so funny?"

It was Caden's voice, and turning around she continued to giggle.

"Caden! What a wonderful surprise. What are you doing here?"

"Max is on death's door apparently, and Richard wanted someone lurkin' around the barn to keep the peace."

"He knows about my argument with Jane?"

"No, I was just kiddin', but he did ask me to hang around and act like a bossman. Somethin' about having the appearance of someone at the helm."

"There's nothing for you to do, at least, I don't think there is. Max is either wandering aimlessly around the barn aisle trying to look busy, or he has his head buried in paperwork in his office."

"That's your observation from one day on the job, is it?"

"Ah, good point," she grinned.

"Why were you laughin' when I came in."

"Here, read this," she said handing him the note.

"Huh, subtle," he said raising his eyebrows.

"The grooms cleaned every bridle, halter and saddle in here yesterday."

"Maybe she didn't notice," Caden suggested.

"Uh, hardly. She and Tim went off on a trail ride, so she would have noticed when she tacked up the horses."

"Not necessarily. The grooms might have done that."

"You're right, they might have. Well, regardless, I'm not cleaning tack that's already been done. Max told me yesterday that he wants me riding in the arena so I can get to know the horses a bit, and that's exactly what I'm going to do."

"Start with Goliath," Caden suggested. "He's the big bay with a diamond on his forehead."

"Okay, Goliath it is," she nodded. "I'll bring him in."

As she picked up a halter and headed out, Caden stared at the note in his hand. It was a full on, frontal attack. Jane wanted to make sure Bridget knew her place. Jane was the boss, and Bridget was her underling.

"I don't see this workin'," he mumbled. "Jane left out all this cleanin' stuff, so she was in here and she would have noticed the job had been done. Damn, this isn't good."

Heading back into the barn aisle, he walked up to one of the workers who was hosing out some buckets.

"Hey, Jimmy, excuse me."

"Hi, Caden. Do you need somethin'?"

"Did Jane and Tim say how long they'd be gone?"

"About an hour or so. They're takin' the trail that goes up the hill behind the house, but when they come back they'll be takin' off again on Duster and Harry. They'll have had the six main trail horses out before lunch."

"Ah, excellent. Could you please help Bridget tack up Goliath. You know which is his saddle and bridle right?"

"Oh, sure, I'm happy to help. She's a real nice girl, that one."

"Yep, she is," Caden nodded, "thanks. I'll go and see what's holdin' her up."

Walking outside he saw Bridget had stopped at the fence of Valentino's paddock. Keeping Goliath behind her, she was stroking Valentino's face, reassuring him that he was her number one, but as she started to leave, Valentino started kicking up a fuss.

"He's jealous," Caden muttered. "Valentino and Bridget are a match. I'll have to work this out somehow. I'm not separatin' them."

She paused, talked to Valentino for a moment longer, then continued on. As she headed towards the barn, he noticed her hair was glimmering red in the sun, and her whole being seemed to be glowing. He was crazy in love with her, and if things with Jane didn't work out, he'd ask her hang out at his ranch and help him with the foals.

"Hey, cowboy," she said as she approached.

"Hey, yourself," he smiled falling into step beside her. "Jane and Tim will be back in about an hour, but they're gonna be takin' out two more. I want you to be in the ring ridin' when they get here, and I want you to stay there until after they leave. I don't want you and Jane havin' words. I want things to settle for a bit."

"Sure, whatever you say," she nodded.

As she led Goliath into the barn, he paused, his eyes scanning the sky. It was a warm day, but as often happened in the spring, he could see storm clouds on the horizon.

"Is that headed our way?" he muttered. "I haven't checked the weather since I got here. I'd better, and I'd better call the ranch, let them know I'll be gone longer than I thought. Bridget," he called stepping into the barn, "I'm just runnin' up to the house for five minutes. I'll be back shortly."

"No worries. Anything I should know about this big guy?"

"Yeah, he stops on a dime. You don't need any rein."

"Glad I asked," she laughed.

She watched him stride away, staring at his wide shoulders and his panther-like walk.

"I am so in love with you, Caden. If Jane, or any woman, comes near you, God help them."

CHAPTER TEN

IT WAS ALMOST MIDDAY, and walking with Caden to her cottage for lunch, Bridget saw a gleaming black Range Rover parked up at the house. She'd heard Heather Chadwick had arrived, but unable to see the front door from the barn, she'd missed catching sight of the star as she'd left the vehicle and moved inside.

The morning had passed with no drama, but it was due to Caden's forward thinking. Every time Jane and Tim were returning from the trail, or leaving to head out again, Bridget was in the ring putting a horse through its paces, and Caden had made sure he and Bridget were on their way to lunch before Jane and Tim returned from their last ride.

"Thanks for making the morning go smoothly," she said as they approached her cabin.

"It was for my benefit too," he said as she opened the door. "Bridget, this is great," he added as he followed her in and scanned the cozy surroundings.

"It is, but I like your suite better."

"Well, sure, but this is very, what's the word?"

"Whimsical?" she suggested. "It's like a getaway place, a gingerbread cottage."

"Yep, that's it."

"Why was it for your benefit too? Keeping the peace this morning, I mean."

"Because I have no desire to break up a cat fight," he said with a grin. "I could get scratched."

"Ha, very funny," she quipped. "Now then, what would you like for lunch? I have many things I can offer you. How about an omelette and a salad?"

"Perfect. I'll make the salad."

"Deal," she agreed. "I have a question."

"Shoot."

"You managed this morning, but what about this afternoon? I want to ride Valentino, but Miss High and Mighty will probably try to stop me. She'll give me some sort of stupid job to do, I'm sure of it."

"I've been thinkin' about that," Caden said solemnly. "I was gonna go into town with Max but I've changed my mind. I'll go in tomorrow. I think I'd better stick around."

"So you can run interference? You don't have to. I can fight my own battles."

"I'm fully aware of that," he said as he began to prepare the lettuce, "but I don't want any battles, not on my watch."

"Then what do you suggest? I'm going to get on Valentino this afternoon, I don't care what she says."

"There's a simple solution. When we go back I'll ask you to ride him for me, then she can't interfere."

"Everything was so nice here, and then she shows up. This sucks," Bridget declared as she began to whisk the eggs.

"Yeah, it kinda does," Caden agreed, "but it might come right. Give it a couple of days and see how it crinkles out. I know Richard is glad you're here. He's been tellin' me for ages that he needed a third horse professional, as he called it."

"I like that," she laughed. "I'm a horse professional. I wonder when we'll meet Heather Chadwick. Do you know which room she's in?"

"No, but we'll probably see her at some point."

"Can we eat in the dining room for dinner?"

"I'm not sure. I'll ask Richard. Technically you're staff, but you're also my guest in the house, so it's a question mark. Our famous Miss Chadwick may not want to mingle."

"Ah, right. I get that. The omelette is going in the pan," she announced.

"Yes ma'am, I'll have this salad ready, and after we eat I'm gonna spank you."

"What? You are not!"

"Yes I am," he chuckled.

"Why?"

"Because you've got a gorgeous butt and the spirit is movin' me, and it just might help keep a lid on that quick tongue of yours if Jane goads you."

"Whip her ass, not mine!"

"You'd be as mad as a bear fightin' for a salmon if I did that."

"Yeah, you're right," she nodded plating the omelette. "Just not too hard. I want to ride, remember?"

"I'll smack your butt as hard as I want, honey," he declared landing a quick swat making her squeal. "Now let's eat."

WHILE CADEN AND BRIDGET were enjoying their lunch, Heather Chadwick was settling into her suite. She loved the ranch, but not because of the horses, or luxurious amenities, or even the isolation, but because they didn't have a two bedroom suite available, and she had a room to herself.

Her mother, Molly Chadwick, was her manager, and solely responsible for Heather's enormous success. Heather was beautiful and talented, but there were hundreds of equally beautiful and talented girls still waiting tables and working as receptionists in production companies. It was Molly that had made the difference.

She had been a penniless, single mother, and when she saw her baby develop with the face of an angel and bubbling energy, she was determined that Heather's looks and effervescent personality would lift them out of poverty. From the time the child was old enough to speak, she was in children's theatre groups, beauty pageants, acting and deportment classes, and at the tender age of six, she'd landed two national commercials. Molly had been able to move them out of their one room studio apartment into much nicer dwellings.

Heather became Molly's job, and Molly was tireless in her efforts. She had run the girl ragged dragging her from one casting office to the next, spending a fortune on her clothes and training, and when it became apparent that Heather had been blessed with celestial singing voice, it had been a tremendous bonus. During dark days when things were not going well, it was the child's voice that convinced Molly pursuing her daughter's fame was God's will. She would shake off her fears and doubts, and emerge from her gloom stronger and more determined than ever.

Molly had not just maintained control over Heather's career, she'd maintained a tight rein on Heather herself. She would not allow her daughter to fall victim to drugs or alcohol, or be exploited by some unemployed, smooth talking, handsome actor looking to ride on her coattails. No, that wasn't going to happen! Molly had decided Heather would marry into wealth, a professional man, a man of taste and breeding, and a man who would support Heather's rising star.

Everything had been going brilliantly. Heather's Oscar win had thrown her into the big leagues. Multi-million dollar offers were walking through the door, and the best and brightest directors wanted to work with her.

Then it happened. Molly's worst nightmare.

Heather fell in love, but not with a man of stature, or even another famous actor. The man in question Molly didn't consider to be a man at all. He was a rock and roll musician, and from the moment Bridget had met him, Molly's control had begun to slip away.

When Jeff Ludlow had stepped in, her sweet, obedient Heather became difficult, suggesting she could choose her own scripts, coming home at all hours, and sometimes not at all. When she'd announced Jeff had asked her to marry him and she'd accepted, Molly knew she had to act. Her years of sacrifice and grueling work were about to blow up, and she would not, could not, allow it.

A short time after the public announcement of the engagement, it was over. The tabloids had a field day, citing everything from infidelity, to Heather's non-existent terrible temper. Though Molly had begged her daughter to tell her what happened, she'd refused, until one night, after many glasses of champagne, Heather confided in the woman who had been there throughout her life, the only person she could trust, and sobbed out her heart.

Her mother was warm and understanding, she held her and rocked her and told her everything would be all right, then booked them into Dudley's Dude Ranch, a place where Jeff Ludlow wouldn't find them. A place where Heather could get some peace, and she would be able to heal her relationship with her daughter.

Heather was happy to leave. Jeff was pestering her, calling and emailing, and though her mother was running interference, Heather was afraid to leave the house for fear of running into him. As the private jet had whisked her out of Burbank Airport, though her heart was still breaking, Heather had managed to hold back her tears, and landing at the small, isolated airstrip, she'd felt her body relax.

She was out of the fray, and she'd find a way to get past the tragedy. The man she absolutely adored, the man she loved with a passion, the man who made her skin sing, and her heart swell with joy, had betrayed her, but she was Heather Chadwick, and she'd get through it.

She'd finished unpacking, and wandering to the window she stared out at the horses lazily grazing. During her teenage years her mother had insisted Heather learn the basics of both dressage and jumping, and Heather had loved every minute. The smell of the barn, the welcoming nicker of her favorite horse, and the thrill of learning, had made her time at the stable her favorite hours of the week.

"I'm going to buy a horse," she mumbled, mesmerized by the view. "That's my priority when I get back to L.A. I'm going to buy a horse and get back into riding. Being around horses will help me, I know it will."

A fresh wave of sadness rattled through her veins, and the heavy tears spilled down her face. Her broken heart was still in tatters, and she was as angry at herself as she was at the man who had betrayed her. Running into the bathroom she splashed her face with cold water, and regaining control she decided on a long, hot bath. Checking the various gels on offer, she selected lavender, and turning on the faucets she dropped several generous dollops into the jacuzzi tub. She was about to undress when the phone called her back to the living room, and she hurried to answer it.

"Hello?"

"Darling, are you settling in?"

"Yes, mother, I'm fine. I'm going to take a lavender bath."

"What a good idea. Are you hungry?"

"No, but after I finish my soak I'd like to go down to the barn and meet the horses."

"Wonderful idea."

"Can you find out when I can ride?"

"Of course. You just call me when you're ready."

"Thanks, mother."

The thought of getting on a horse again sent a half-smile to her lips, and stopping by the window for a last look, the smile grew wider.

"You'll help mend me," she murmured. "I know you will. I should never have stopped riding. I'm going to buy a horse, and care for it and ride whenever I can. No, not whenever I can, no. I'm going to make sure any contract I sign allows me time to be at the barn."

BACK IN BRIDGET'S CABIN, she and Caden had just finished their lunch, and Bridget was clearing up the dishes.

"Why don't we go for a walk after we wash these up," she suggested.

"We could," Caden replied casually, standing up to help her, "but there's something I need to take care of first."

"Really?" she said airily. "What would that be?"

"You're adorable," he chuckled. "You know what I'm talking about."

"I do?"

"You keep playin' coy like that and I might take it into my head to add a few extra swats," he warned placing the dishes he'd been carrying on the counter.

"You don't need to spank me again," she protested. "My ass is still tender from before!"

"This is what's gonna happen," he said calmly, taking her hands. "You ready? You listenin'?"

"I'm listening," she sighed.

"I'm gonna go into the bedroom. You're gonna finish cleanin' up, then you're gonna come in, kneel in front of me, and ask me to spank you."

"I am?"

"Yep."

"Why?"

"Why?" he laughed. "Did you just ask me why?"

"I did."

"I've already told you the why, and, darlin'," he said dropping his voice, "you'd best not ask me again. When you're back at the ranch, you're gonna spend a couple of days in trainin', and that means bein' in the house dressed in a skirt with no panties. I'm gonna be liftin' that skirt and whackin' that butt whenever I feel like it, and if you ask me why every time, it's gonna get real red, real fast."

"Oh," she whispered, *why did that make me so hot. Good grief, I want him to jump my bones right now.*

"Don't keep me waitin' too long," he said firmly. "Now kiss me."

Lifting her arms around his neck, she tilted up her chin, and moved her mouth across his. He held her softly, kissing her back with a warmth and tenderness that sent her butterflies dancing, and when she pulled back, she stared into his sparkling blue eyes.

"I love you so much, Caden."

"I love you so much too, sweet girl. Are you gonna do as you're told?"

"Absolutely," she breathed.

Giving her a hug, he headed into the bedroom. His cock had risen to life, and pulling off his boots and jeans he sat on the edge of the bed. He'd only been there a minute or two when Bridget walked in the door. She hesitated for a moment, then moved across and dropped to her knees.

"Please, Sir, will you spank me?"

"Why do you want me to spank you, Bridget?"

"Uh, because I know you want to, and..."

"And?"

"Because I want you to, Sir. It helps me stay centered, and it, uh, just helps me."

"Even though I make your bottom sting?"

"Yes, Sir."

"Drop your jeans and panties to your knees, keep your feet on the floor and bend over my lap."

Sliding down her zipper, her butterflies flew into a frenzy, but as she stretched herself over his lap, she let out a long, grateful sigh.

"I thought so," he remarked moving his hand over her cheeks. "You may debate me, but in the end you need this."

"I do, Sir," she bleated.

"No matter what Jane says or does when we get back to the barn, you'll smile, and nod, and play nice, understood?"

"Yes, Sir."

"I do want you to enjoy your ride, so I won't spank you too hard, just enough to make sure you do as I say."

Before she could respond his hand went to work, but rather than cover her entire seat, he focused on her sensitive sit spot.

"Gonna make sure you remember this when you sit in that saddle," he said sternly.

"Ow, Ow, oh, Sir, Ow, I will. Ouch."

"Shush, just a few more," he said pausing. "Not a sound. Let's see just how obedient you can be."

Bridget grabbed a pillow and grit her teeth as he went back to work. His hand had slowed, but it was landing harder smacks, and just when she thought she could no longer contain herself, it stopped.

"I'm proud of you," he crooned as his hand began to rub away the burn. "You'll get a reward for that."

"Thank you, Sir," she panted.

"My goodness, aren't you wet?" he murmured slipping a finger into her open channel. "I'm gonna rub you to a lovely release for bein' such a good girl and not makin' a sound."

"Oh, thank you, Sir," she mewled wriggling against his hand.

"One thing you'll learn, darlin', if you're good, you'll be rewarded, and if you're bad, you'll be punished. Relax now, and let it happen."

Sinking into his wide, strong lap, Bridget closed her eyes and let the moment build. He was frigging her, then rubbing her clit, and when his free hand moved under her body and tweaked her nipple, it sent a shard of electricity sparking through her body.

"I'm so close," she moaned.

"I know, baby, don't chase, just let it happen."

He tweaked her nipple again, but harder, and his finger working her cunt increased its pace. She could feel her moment hovering, then suddenly the delicious eruption washed through her.

Caden watched her, relishing the sight, continuing his attention until the moment had passed, then he shifted her on to the bed and pulled off her T-shirt. Dropping his briefs, he kneeled above her, and gazing down at her glorious body, her jeans still around her legs, he massaged himself to a deep and satisfying climax.

He stayed there for a moment, catching his breath, then moving from the bed he made his way into the bathroom, washed up, then flopped on the bed next to her.

"Ready to face the afternoon?" he crooned bringing her into his arms.

"So ready," she sighed snuggling next to him.

"You did those dishes really fast."

"Nope, they're in the sink. I couldn't stand it. I had to come in."

"I see," he said smiling. "I'll have to think about that."

"No, you won't," she giggled.

"No," he chuckled, "no, I won't."

"How much time do we have?"

"Let's see, about twenty minutes. Why?"

"Because I'm so happy right now, and I just want to lay here with you."

"That works for me. Did you hear there's a storm on its way?"

"No," she yawned. "When is it coming?"

"Tomorrow some time, maybe late mornin', early afternoon, could be any time I guess."

"Huh. Should we bring in the horses?"

"I'm thinkin' so, just in case it gets squally."

"I can't wait to see your ranch."

"You'll love it," he sighed.

"I can't wait to walk around in a skirt with no underwear," she whispered.

"Is that so? You think about that and nap now. I need to catch five minutes," he yawned.

"Mmm, okay."

As Caden let himself unwind, his mind wandered to his basement, a space he'd outfitted over the last few years, piece by piece, implement by implement. He'd only allowed two other people down there, close friends who were in a domestic discipline marriage. After their visit they'd built their own basement playroom. He smiled. He couldn't wait.

CHAPTER ELEVEN

"LET ME DO ALL THE TALKIN'," Caden said as he and Bridget approached the barn.

"Happily," she quipped. "I'll just walk in and grab a halter. I'd much rather be in Valentino's company than Jane's."

"Should I have spanked you with a bit more gusto?" he asked lowering his voice.

"No! I'll play nice, I promise."

Entering the barn aisle, Tim came walking briskly forward, smiling happily.

"Hey, Caden, and you're obviously Bridget, I've yet to officially meet you. Welcome."

"Oh, uh, hi," Bridget replied somewhat taken aback by the young man's warmth.

"Glad to have an extra hand," he continued. "If you have any questions, please feel free. The horses are all great, mainly because of this man here."

"Nice of you to say, thanks," Caden replied. "Where's Jane?"

"Jane? She's gone into town with Richard."

"No wonder you're in such a good mood," Bridget muttered under her breath.

"Sorry?" Tim said. "I didn't catch that."

"I said, I wonder why you're in such a good mood," Bridget said quickly. "You know, being the first day back and everything."

"I'm enjoyin' the quiet before the storm. This place will be full in a few days, and things will be buzzin' around here," he replied. "I wanted to ask you, Caden, Jane said that chestnut geldin' won't be stayin'? Is that right? Sure is a good lookin' horse."

"Not sure what I'll be doin' with him just yet."

"I'm getting on him now if you want to watch," Bridget said.

"Yeah, I do. I'm done for the day, but I heard you're gonna be ridin' in the ring through the afternoon. Some days, we just work with the horses in the mornin' and we're done by lunch, other days we're busy with clients all day and into the evenin'."

"I understand, I think most barns are like that. I'm used to it. I'm going to get Valentino."

Relieved that Jane wasn't around, Bridget picked up a halter and headed out, and as she strode across the stable yard to the paddock, she was unaware that watching from her window, Heather's eyes were following her.

Heather had been admiring the big, glossy, chestnut gelding for some time, mesmerized by his glimmering coat and his elegant movement. Bridget approached the fence, and Heather watched as the big gelding broke into a trot, clearly excited to see the auburn-haired girl at the gate. The girl slipped the halter over his head and led the horse back towards the barn. Immediately reaching for the phone, Heather called her mother.

"Hello?"

"Mother, I know you wanted to lay by the pool before we went to the barn, but I'm going there now. There's a horse I want to see, He's just being brought in from its paddock. I'm going to run down there."

"Wait for me, I'm coming to your room."

Dressed in light cotton slacks, a lemon silk shirt and ballet slippers, Heather realized she needed to change, and by the time her mother knocked on her door she was in jeans, boots and a T-shirt.

"Heather, you look like a hillbilly. I didn't even know you owned clothes like that."

"I'm going to a stable, mother. These are barn clothes."

Jeff had bought them for her, and though she didn't understand why she'd brought them with her, she was glad she had.

"You still have an image to maintain," her mother remarked.

"I thought we came here so I could forget about all that."

"You're right, I'm sorry, it's just the way my mind works. Anyway, Celeste is taking us down there in a golf cart."

"Super. Let's go."

"What's so special about this horse?" Molly asked as they started down the hallway.

"He's so beautiful. I've been watching him for the last half hour. He's a gorgeous chestnut with two white stockings on his back legs, and a diamond on his forehead. Mother, I've decided I want to start riding again. More than that, I want to buy my own horse."

"Bridget, I applaud that idea," Molly beamed, thrilled it might keep her mind of scruffy musicians. "Yes, that would be excellent for you. We'll sort that out the minute we get back and we should join a Polo Club as well," she added, thinking it would be the perfect place for her to meet an eligible bachelor.

"I'd love that, yes, we should," Heather agreed.

Delighted her daughter was suddenly so buoyant, Molly felt the tension beginning to leave her neck.

"Hello," Celeste said, greeting them as they descended the stairs. "The golf car is just outside."

"Thank you. Heather has just told me there's a horse here she's quite taken with," Molly declared as Celeste ushered them through the door. "Do you know his name, Heather?"

"No, but mother, he'll be in the barn when we get there."

"You said he was a chestnut, didn't you?"

"Yes, with two white stockings and a diamond," Heather replied as she sat in the back seat of the cart.

"That must be Valentino," Celeste said as she started down the driveway. "He's just arrived. I'm not sure if he's staying or not. He doesn't belong to us, at least, not yet."

They pulled into the stable yard just in time to see Caden give Bridget a boost into the saddle, and jumping from the cart, Heather stood and stared at the big gleaming chestnut.

"My gosh, he's amazing," she mumbled. "He's the most beautiful horse I've ever seen. He's so much bigger than I thought."

Settled in the saddle, Bridget glanced towards the cart, and was shocked to see the famous star and her mother. She'd heard it approach, but had assumed it was Richard, and not wanting to make eye contact with Jane she'd kept her gaze lowered. Tim, standing back in the shadows, stayed where he was. He'd learned that celebrities preferred to be the ones to make the first move.

"Caden," Bridget said quietly, "look, it's Heather Chadwick."

Turning around Caden saw the stunning blond standing by the cart staring at them, and immediately walked forward to introduce himself. Not sure what to do, and not wanting to gawk, Bridget headed to the riding ring.

"Caden," Celeste said stepping towards him, "I'd like you to meet Heather Chadwick and her mother, Molly. Heather, Molly, this is Caden Price. He's the man who finds us all our fabulous horses, and keeps them that way."

"Hello, Caden. That chestnut, what an incredible looking horse," she remarked, thinking Caden was just as handsome.

"Nice to meet you, Caden," Molly said formally.

"That's Valentino, and Bridget, the girl sitting on him, she's about to ride him in the ring if you want to watch."

"Yes, definitely, I'd love to," Heather said enthusiastically.

"Follow me, we have a viewing deck," Caden said.

"Before you go, tell me, Caden, who's in charge of the barn?"

"That would be Max, but he's out sick, so I'm stepping in until he's better, and a young woman named Jane is his assistant. She's not here right now."

"Ah, good, well, thank you. Heather, you go ahead dear, it's a bit dusty out there for me. I'll just wait for you."

"You don't have to do that. Go back to the house, have some coffee, or tea or something. You're not dressed to be at a barn anyway."

"Hmm, I'm not sure."

"You can see the arena from the hotel terrace if that's of any help," Celeste suggested.

"Oh, then yes, that's what I'll do," Molly declared. "I'll have some coffee and watch from up there. That will be much more comfortable. Thank you, Celeste."

Bridget was walking around, letting Valentino settle, but she'd been watching the scene play out in the stable yard. When Heather's mother left in the golf cart, and Heather started walking towards the ring next to Caden, she forced herself not to feel jealous or insecure, but it wasn't easy. The girl was as gorgeous as her television and movie appearances promised. Not wanting them to see her staring, Bridget looked ahead and asked Valentino to step into the trot, and as the horse picked up the gait, she could feel the sting on her seat. It sent a warm reassurance to her heart, and she felt herself begin to relax.

As she continued around the ring she saw them sit down, but as she started down the long side, which would take her right past them, Caden rose to his feet and waved her over. Asking Valentino to slow to a walk, she approached the viewing platform.

"Bridget," Caden said with a broad smile, "this is Heather Chadwick, Heather, this is Bridget Cooper. Bridget is not just a fabulous rider, she's also the reason I have a big smile on my face when I wake up in the mornin.'"

Surprised by his sweet comment, for a moment she didn't know what to say, then it came to her.

"Not as big as mine!" she declared with a wink. "Hi, Heather, nice to meet you."

"You too," Heather replied. "You guys are so lucky. I'd love wake up with a smile like that." *I did, for a short time anyway.* "Hello, Valentino. Aren't you a handsome horse?"

"Isn't he though, and he's such a lover," Bridget remarked.

"I'm dying to see him go," Heather said. "Please, don't let me stop you."

"This is only the second time I've ridden him and I'm going to try some fancy footwork, so I can't promise it will be perfect."

"Just watching him is perfect," Heather sighed.

"Hey," Caden said leaning over the railing, "wait a second. Come closer to the rail."

Bridget moved Valentino next to the fence, and to her shock, Caden leaned over and kissed her on the cheek.

"Just 'cos," he winked.

Walking away from the viewing deck, she felt a deep warmth fill her heart. He'd guessed she might feel uneasy with the famous beauty beside him, and he'd gone out of his way to reassure her.

Exhilarated, she pushed Valentino into an extended trot, then a canter, and a gallop, then brought him back to a walk. Taking a moment to catch her breath, she asked him for more advanced maneuvers, and he had no problem understanding her requests, performing the intricate steps and turns flawlessly.

She'd been so focused on her riding she hadn't noticed Celeste had returned in the golf cart, but as she started trotting over to ask Caden for his feedback, she saw Celeste driving the cart to the viewing platform and urgently gesturing for Caden to join her. By the time she'd reached the fence, he and Celeste were deep in conversation.

"Caden! Is everything all right?" she asked as Caden broke away and started towards her.

"I have an emergency phone call from my ranch. I think it's one of the mares. I'm runnin' into the barn to take it."

"Oh, no. I'll come right in."

"No, you stay here and chat with Heather. I'll be right back. That was fantastic by the way, you two looked great."

"Thanks. Shoot. I hope everything's okay."

"Me too," he frowned jumping into the cart.

"He has a ranch?" Heather asked.

"Yes, about forty-five minutes away. He has a breeding program there, and he also trains and sells top quality horses. Valentino belongs to him."

"Really? That's interesting. All kinds of horses, or just western horses."

"All kinds. That man can do anything. Don't let his cowboy hat fool you. I've seen him jump fences flawlessly on warmbloods and thoroughbreds, then do team penning and roping on a quarter-horse."

"That's impressive," Heather declared. "I've never ridden in a western saddle. Is it much different?"

"It is. It probably wouldn't take long for you to adapt, but you might not like it."

"Do you give lessons here?"

"Yes, but I just started, and I'm not sure how things work. I'd love to help you. I'll find out."

"That would be fantastic," Heather said eagerly. "Look, Caden's coming back."

"Shoot, he doesn't look very happy."

Celeste had returned him in the cart, and jumping out he walked briskly up the stairs to the viewing platform.

"I have to go. One of my mares is havin' her baby and ran into trouble. The vet's on the way. He'll beat me there but I need to get home."

"Caden, I'm so sorry. I'll come with you," Bridget said earnestly.

"No, you stay here. I'll call you later, and hopefully I'll be back in the mornin."

"How are you getting there? You're not taking the horse van, are you?"

"No, I'll take one of the ranch cars."

"Caden, I'm sorry," Heather interjected.

"Thank you Heather. Hopefully it will work out. Sorry I have to dash. Bye, darlin," he said turning to Bridget. "I promise I'll call you soon, oh, and my suite is unlocked if you want to stay up there."

"Okay, thanks, Caden. Please drive carefully."

"I will. Bye."

Wishing she was leaving with him, Bridget watched him trot down the steps, climb into the cart and race away.

"Bummer," Heather remarked.

"Yeah, major bummer," Bridget nodded. "I'm worried."

"Me too. Will you let me know what's going on when you hear from him? I mean it. That poor mare. I want to know, I really do."

"Yes, sure."

"I'm in room 108."

"You are? Caden's staying in 107."

"What about you?"

"I'm in a little cabin at the back of the property, but I might stay in his suite tonight. I'm not sure, the cabin is cozy and has a full kitchen and-"

"Why don't you stay in 107?" Heather interrupted. "We could get together, have a drink or something, you know, later, after I finish having dinner with my mother. I'd really like to talk to you about horses."

"Uh, sure, if you want."

"I do, I really do."

"Then it's a date," Bridget smiled. "I need to walk Valentino out for five minutes, then I'll be taking him back to the barn."

Rising to her feet, Heather stared up at the terrace. Her mother waved, but didn't gesture for her to come back.

"Can I join you?" Heather asked.

"Of course," Bridget smiled, then looking into the eyes of the beautiful star, it hit her. *Oh, my, gosh, you're lonely.*

"Thanks," Heather smiled. "It's been too long since I've been close to a horse and stroked its neck."

"You can stroke his neck all you want, he'd love it," Bridget assured her. "Okay, Mister Valentino, let's get walkin'."

A short time later, as Bridget watched Heather groom Valentino, the young star's passion for horses and riding became obvious. She smiled and laughed, and talked to Valentino with joy in her voice, but as they parted company, Bridget saw a cloud of sadness descend around her.

"She seems okay for a superstar," Tim remarked walking up to stand beside her.

"There you are! Yes, she is, she's very okay," Bridget replied. "Where did you disappear to?"

"I watched you ride from the other side of the ring. You're really good, Bridget, and that horse, damn. Did he show a lot?"

"He must have. He's so finely tuned."

"I could tell."

"Why didn't you join us?" Bridget asked. "Where have you been?"

"Jane likes to be the one to deal with the guests," he replied. "Things go a lot smoother around here if you let her be. Just keep your head down, do as she says, and you won't have any problems."

"I see," she said grimly. "That's okay with you?"

"I love this place. It's a great job and I wanna keep it, so, yeah, it's okay with me, besides, nothin' lasts forever."

Bridget narrowed her eyes. The comment had buzzed her radar.

"What do you mean?"

"Nothin'. Just what I've noticed workin' at ranches. People come and go."

"You're right," she agreed, though she was sensing more behind his comment. "I doubt I'll be here very long. I'm not interested in being a wallflower, and Jane and I got off to a rocky start."

"Yeah, that doesn't surprise me."

"It doesn't?"

"No, but hey, I hope you do stick around. You brighten up the place. I'm headin' home for a nap. Been up since six."

"Why so early?"

"Jane wanted us to start by seven, so..."

"I see."

"Oh, that reminds me. She'll page you tonight and tell you what time to report in tomorrow. With only one guest here there won't be much to do. We have a list of who's comin' in and when, and we get the horses ready the day before they arrive."

"Ah, good to know, and if I don't hear from her?"

"That's up to you," he grinned.

"Got it," she laughed. "I'll put Valentino back in his paddock and get on the next one."

"Okay. Catch ya!"

Taking Valentino from the cross ties, she fed him some carrots, then led him out to his pasture. He seemed serene and happy, and as she took off his halter, he didn't turn and walk away as the other horses had done, but stayed with her, lowering his head to her chest for attention.

"Valentino, you're such a special guy. I do adore you. No, I take that back. I've fallen in love with you."

He nickered softly, then gave her a gentle nudge.

"Did you just say you love me too? Oh, sweet horse, I believe you did."

CHAPTER TWELVE

THE SUN WAS LOW IN the sky, and after packing an overnight bag, Bridget headed up to Caden's room, dying for a soak in his large, jacuzzi tub. The big house seemed quiet as she walked up the stairs and let herself into his suite, and tired and dusty from the busy afternoon, she moved straight into the bathroom. Choosing some jasmine bath gel, she turned on the faucets and dropped several large dollops into the tub, then peeled off her dirty, dusty clothes. Stuffing her hair under a shower cap, she slid into the foamy water, closed her eyes, and sinking into the comforting warmth, she let out a long grateful sigh.

"I hope Caden's mare is okay. Poor thing. I wish I was there with him. Heather's a poor thing too," she mumbled. "I wonder what's making her so sad. That mother of hers is a trip. Good grief. Talk about a prima donna, and she seems like a total control freak. Caden, I miss you. Training. That's what you said. God, that turns me on! That thing about wearing a skirt so you can lift it and smack me..."

Her hand slipped between her legs, but recalling his edict, moaning reluctantly, she pulled it away.

"It's not fair! I should be allowed to do this. I'd be totally focused on you and all your wicked promises."

Resigning herself to a simple soak, she forced herself to think about things other than her sexy cowboy and his salacious plans. Finally rising from the tub, she toweled off, donned the bathrobe hanging on the hook behind the door, and was walking into the bedroom when the phone rang. Running to answer it, praying it was Caden, she picked up the receiver.

"Hello?"

"Hey, darlin.'"

His voice sounded weary, but not sad or melancholy.

"How is she?" Bridget asked hoping she'd read him correctly.

"It was touch and go, but she's out of the woods, and I have a brand new foal. A little girl. Cute as could be."

"Yay. Silly question, but aren't they all cute?"

"Yes, Bridget, they are, but some are cuter than others. I can already tell she'll be full of mischief. Her mother is, so it's in her blood."

"She's really okay, the mother?"

"Patty, yes, but I'm stayin' here overnight just in case."

"Do you have cameras in the barn so you can monitor her?"

"Oh, sure, but I'm not relyin' on that. I'll bring a sleepin' bag down here and stay in the stall next to her and her baby."

"Really?"

"I'm not leavin' her, not a chance. The vet said she'd should be brighter in the mornin', and as long as she is I can head on back there."

"Caden, you take my breath away. That is so wonderful."

"What?"

"Sleeping in the stall to watch over her. I wish I was there with you."

"Me too, but I think she's gonna be just fine and we'll be together again tomorrow. What's goin' on there? How was Heather?"

"She's so nice, Caden. She helped me clean up Valentino, and she wants to take a lesson. I have to check with Richard and find out how that works. The only thing is…"

"Is what?"

"I think she's really sad."

"Of course she is."

"I don't understand."

"Didn't you hear about her and Jeff Ludlow?"

"They're engaged right? Did something happen? Is that why she's here with her mother and not him?"

"You honestly don't know?"

"No, tell me. I don't watch those entertainment shows. What?"

"The engagement was called off, and it wasn't that long ago, maybe, two, three weeks?"

"I wonder why," Bridget frowned. "At least that explains it. I'm glad you told me. She asked if she could come over and have a drink with me tonight, after she's had dinner with her mother."

"Probably wants some normal company."

"I'm sure," Bridget agreed, "and to talk about horses. Um, Caden?"

"Yes, darlin', what's that I'm hearin' in your voice?"

"I was wondering, can I, uh, please may I have permission to play with myself?"

"No, I don't think so."

"No? Why not?"

"I have my reasons."

"Can I know what they are?"

"When I get back."

"What if I beg?"

"Beggin' can be good, but it won't change my mind."

"Shoot."

"Have you seen Jane?"

"No, she was MIA all afternoon. You didn't need to spank me at lunchtime after all."

"Darlin'," he said lowering his voice, "you always need to be spanked."

"Oh, Caden, please, can I touch myself? Pleeease?"

"You can, of course you can, but then I'll have to punish you, and that doesn't necessarily mean a spankin'."

"What does it mean then?"

"Disobey me and find out," he warned. "Just so we're clear, I'm tellin' you, no you may not touch yourself. Understand?"

"Yes, Sir," she breathed feeling the slick heat between her legs.

"I'm gonna go now. I need to eat and have some coffee. Don't worry if I don't call you tonight. I'm exhausted. I'll probably fall asleep early, but I promise I'll call you in the mornin'."

"Okay. I love you and miss you," she said wistfully.

"Back at ya, darlin'."

Hanging up the phone, she leaned back on the bed, grabbed a pillow and hugged it to her chest. She couldn't believe he was sleeping in a stall next to his mare!

"I think I just fell in love with you all over again. I'm so tired. Maybe I'll take a quick nap."

Drifting off to images of Caden and Valentino, she had disjointed dreams of them both, and when she blinked open her eyes she was shocked to see it had passed seven o'clock. Wide awake and hungry, not wanting to intrude on Heather and her mother in the dining room, she called down for some dinner, then dressed in case Heather should knock on her door.

As she waited for her meal, staring out at the quickly darkening sky, she realized she hadn't called Richard about giving Heather a lesson.

"Shoot, it's too late now. I'll call him first thing in the morning," she muttered, "and I didn't get a page from Jane. Maybe I slept through it."

Moving across to the desk she picked up her pager.

"Nothing. Huh, maybe she's just going to ignore me. A girl like that, who knows what she'll do. I knew she'd be trouble."

Dinner arrived, and she ate it slowly, enjoying every bite. She'd ordered a bottle of wine, not to have with her meal, but because she wanted it there to share with Heather when she arrived, and as she put the tray outside her door for room service to collect, she saw the young star walking towards her.

"Hi," Bridget smiled.

"Looks like good timing," Heather remarked.

"Perfect, I just finished dinner. Come on in."

"The food here is ridiculous," Heather said walking into the suite.

"I know, not that I've eaten in many high-end places, but I think it's great."

"My mother is impossible to please, but even she's raving."

"Wine?" Bridget offered, thinking Heather seemed edgy.

"You bet. I can't drink around my mother," Heather said moving around the room, "unless I'm upset, then she doesn't seem to mind."

"You can have whatever you want here," Bridget declared pouring them both a glass.

Taking it from her, Heather took a swallow, then stood for minute, looking uncomfortable.

"This is lovely," she said. "Whoever decorated this place did a terrific job."

"I agree," Bridget nodded. *Why are you so nervous? Hmm, should I ask?*

"I like how all the rooms face the paddocks," Heather continued.

"Heather," Bridget said slowly, "I get the feeling you want to talk to me about something. I don't mean to pry, but-"

"It's just..." she began, then taking another swallow of wine she wandered to the window, and staring out across the grounds, she muttered, "the landscaping lights are gorgeous."

"It's just?" Bridget pressed.

"Sorry," Heather sighed. "It was seeing you and Caden today."

"What about us?"

"You're so happy," she said wistfully.

"I'm sorry about you and Jeff Ludlow," Bridget said quietly.

"It's really hard," Bridget mumbled. "Sorry. I don't know why, but I feel like I can talk to you."

"Of course you can," Bridget said warmly, "and I'm glad you feel that way."

"Maybe it's the horse thing. Being with you and Valentino today was incredible. It really cheered me up."

"Horses do that for me too. They're my therapy. They make everything okay."

"I know, right?" Heather agreed. "It's their energy or something. I really miss being around them, but I'm going to change that. I'm definitely getting back into riding."

"I couldn't live without horses in my life. If it's in your blood, you can't stay away from them. Even if you take a break, you have to get back to them."

"Its definitely in me," Heather nodded. "I felt so much better when I was with you in the barn."

"Maybe you and Jeff can work things out," Bridget suggested.

"I don't think so."

"About two months ago, I walked away from Caden, and it was horrible. I felt as if someone had punched me in the gut, it hurt so bad."

"You left him? Why?"

"I saw him with another woman. Before I started going out with him, he had a reputation for being a total player, so I immediately assumed he was cheating on me."

"Oh, my, gosh. That's happening with me," Heather exclaimed. "How did you get past it? I mean, if he cheated on you..."

"It turned out that he hadn't. The girl who used to own Valentino had to give him up, and she'd just handed him over to Caden. She was really upset, and Caden was just comforting her."

"You jumped to the wrong conclusion."

"Totally. We just got back together a couple of days ago."

"That recently? Why did it take so long?"

"I refused to talk to him," Bridget said frowning. "I was such an idiot. He finally got me to listen to him. I won't bore you with how that happened, but honestly, I thought we were totally done, and now look.

You never know what might happen. Maybe there's more hope for you and Jeff than you think."

"I doubt it," Heather muttered swallowing a fresh wave of sadness.

"You just said the same thing happened to you. Maybe you misunderstood like I did," Bridget offered. "Can you talk about it?"

"There's not much to talk about. One day I opened up my email, and there was a photograph of him and some girl in bed together."

"What? That's crazy Who sent it?"

"I have no idea. After I told my mother she hired a private detective but they couldn't trace where the email came from. He had a new haircut, so I knew the picture had just been taken. I forwarded it to him, and told him we were done," she finished, tears abruptly spilling down her face.

"Oh, Heather, this sounds crazy."

"It was, totally crazy," she sputtered.

"This is horrible."

"He emailed me back, he said he had no idea what it was, but I wouldn't listen, I mean, how could I? He was there, with another woman, in color. After that he starting calling me, leaving me messages saying he hadn't done anything, begging me to let him tell his side of the story, but I couldn't handle it. I didn't need to hear lies and excuses."

"I know that feeling," Bridget remarked.

"I got a new phone with a different number, and a new email, and my mother wouldn't let him in the door, then she decided to bring me here, so Jeff wouldn't be able to pester me."

"That's so weird, that's exactly why I came here, so Caden couldn't reach me, and I wouldn't have to risk running into him. This is totally bizarre," Bridget declared shaking her head.

"Really? That is weird," Heather nodded wiping the tears from her face. "Wait a second, he was here? How did he find you?"

"I'll tell you about that later. It's just so bizarre that you're going through almost exactly the same thing I did."

"It is," Heather frowned. "It totally is, except I have photographs. Oh, I can't stand to think about it."

"Don't you think what happened to you and Jeff is a bit strange?" Bridget said thoughtfully.

"How do you mean?"

"It must have been right after you announced your engagement, right?"

"Just a few days."

"Why would anyone do that to you? How would they get your email, and a story like that, whoever it was could have sold it to the tabloids for a mint, couldn't they, especially with racy pictures?"

"Huh," Heather said with a heavy frown. "I guess I never thought about it. I just reacted."

"Maybe I'm crazy, but it reeks of someone purposely sabotaging you two."

"Who would do that, and why," Heather said drinking her wine, then looking very sad, she added, "and does it make any difference? He did what he did."

"Are you sure? I keep thinking about what happened to me and Caden. It looked so bad, but it wasn't. Heather, what exactly did the picture show."

"Jeff was naked, or rather, his lower half was covered by a blanket, his eyes were closed, and this girl in this really trashy lingerie was lying next to him."

"That's it?"

"That's not enough?" Heather declared downing another swallow of wine.

"Were there other pictures, or just one?"

"There were three, all similar, except one where the girl's eyes were open."

"I'm going to give you some advice," Bridget said soberly, "advice I wish someone had given me. Call Jeff, listen to what he has to say. I've got a funny feeling about all this."

Heather stared at her, then walked across to a chair and dropped down.

"You think it was a setup," Heather murmured, her voice almost a whisper. "You think he had no idea what was happening. You think the whole thing was done deliberately to break us up."

"Yeah," Bridget nodded, "I think it's at least a possibility. Do you know anyone who would have wanted to do that? Someone who knew your email address, and could finagle something complicated like that?"

"Only one person," Heather breathed staring at her hands. "I'm afraid to call Jeff, because if you're right, there's no good outcome."

"What do you mean?"

"Either Jeff really was in bed with another woman, or it was my mother's handiwork. Like I said, no good outcome."

"Shit. I'm really sorry," Bridget muttered walking across to her. "I should have kept my big mouth shut."

"No. No, that's not true. I had such a weird feeling when it happened, and I didn't know why it seemed so...off...somehow. Everything you just asked, who would have my email, why didn't they just sell the pictures, and one question that just came into my head, who would be in a position to even take a picture like that?"

"You need to talk to him," Bridget reiterated. "At least hear what he has to say."

"You're right," Heather nodded staring at her. "So strange that I should meet you, and you were here to help me like this."

"It is, but it's good strange," Bridget smiled.

"Very good strange," Heather agreed. "I'll call him tomorrow after my lesson. I'm not sure I can face it tonight."

"Lesson? Do you mean a riding lesson?"

"Yes. My mother arranged it. I guess Jane has to evaluate me before she can let me take a lesson with you."

"I see."

"I told mother I didn't want to take a lesson with Jane, I wanted it to be with you, but Jane told her it was the hotel policy and it had to do with insurance or something."

"When are you having this lesson?"

"Tomorrow morning at ten-thirty. She said it would take about an hour. I'm excited, but I wish it was going to be with you. Will you come down and watch."

"Maybe. I can always watch from the terrace."

"Can't you come and sit on the viewing deck?"

"Let me think about it. Like I said, I just started here, and I don't want to step on anybody's toes."

"I can tell her I insisted you be there, or would that be difficult for you?"

"It might be, let me think about it, and my goodness, I forgot to tell you. I talked to Caden. The mare is doing better. He's staying overnight just in case, but he should be back here tomorrow morning."

"That's fabulous, what a relief," Heather smiled.

"Listen to this," Bridget said dramatically. "He's taking a sleeping bag into the stall next to her, so he can be right there with her and the baby through the night."

"Ooh, no wonder you're so in love with him."

"He's the best," Bridget sighed. "The foal is a little girl, by the way."

"That news has really perked me up," Heather declared. "I've felt weird about this whole thing with Jeff from the very beginning. I'm definitely calling him tomorrow, and one way or another, I'm getting the truth, whatever that truth may be."

"Good for you," Bridget exclaimed. "You won't rest if you don't."

"Here's to new beginnings," Heather said raising her glass.

"New beginnings," Bridget said clinking.

"Did you hear we might be having a storm tomorrow?"

"I did," Bridget replied.

"I know this old character actor. He told me once that a storm blows in change. There's the drama of the thunder and lightening, the rain to wash everything clean, and then the dawn of a new day."

"That sounds profound and accurate," Bridget declared.

"I'm so grateful to you," Heather sighed. "Thank you for everything."

"I didn't do very much," Bridget replied, "but you're welcome."

"The thing is," Heather began tentatively, "when I met you, you treated me like a normal human being, and so did Caden. I hope we can stay friends after we leave here."

"I'd like that," Bridget said warmly. "Now I think we'd better finish off this wine before we get too mushy. Shall we order up some rich, decadent dessert?"

"Yes!" Heather said eagerly. "Mother scowls at me when I do that."

"No scowling from me, but I might fight you for the last bite," Bridget laughed.

It was some time later that Heather hugged Bridget goodbye, and made her way slowly to her suite. Bridget watched from her door to make sure she got there safely, then staggering into the bedroom she collapsed on the bed.

"What a night, and tomorrow is going to be a helluva day," she said with a weary sigh. "I hope Caden gets back in time for her lesson. I'm right about that Jeff thing. I can feel it. Man, I'm sooo tired. Goodnight, Caden, goodnight Valentino, good night, mare and foal, good night my new friend, Heather. God bless you all."

CHAPTER EIGHTEEN

EARLY THE FOLLOWING afternoon, after accepting a lunch invitation from Heather and Jeff, Caden headed to Celeste's office to return the key to Jane's cottage, while Bridget returned to the suite to pick up her handbag. Their suitcases were already in the horse van down at the barn. All they had to do was load Valentino and they could leave. Approaching Celeste's door, he gave a little knock and walked in, and to his delight he saw a dozen red roses in a crystal glass vase, and a large box of unopened chocolates sitting on her desk.

"What's this?" he asked with a grin.

"Uh, from Richard," she said shyly.

"That old fox," he laughed. "I've already said my goodbyes to him, so I'll refrain from stickin' my head in to razz him."

"Please do," she begged. "I think sending me these things was very difficult. He hasn't been able to look me in the eye all day."

"He'll get there. He's just catchin' his breath," Caden assured her. "The key was a big help, thanks, Celeste. I'll be back soon."

Leaning over her desk he pecked her on the cheek, then walking back into the foyer he found Bridget waiting.

"Ready?"

"Yes," she nodded.

"Let's take the golf cart," he suggested. "You still need to take things easy."

"Please, I can walk to the barn," she scoffed.

"You either come in the golf cart, or I'll pick you up in the van on the way out."

"Fine," she sighed. "I'll come with you in the cart."

Five minutes later Caden was loading Valentino into the horse van, and with a last goodbye and thank you to Tim, he and Bridget set off for his ranch.

The day was idyllic. Spotty clouds and warm sunshine made the drive picturesque, and when Caden turned off the main road, driving through a small town much like the one near Dudley's Dude Ranch, it was a short distance to the tree lined lane leading up to his house.

If the appearance of Dudley's had surprised Bridget when she'd first seen it, Caden's house was equally startling. She'd thought it would be a sprawling, one level ranch home, but she was met by a two-story, log house with double-story front windows. A natural grey brick front patio, and a chimney made of the same stone, gave the home an elegant appearance, and glancing across at him she broke into a smile.

"Caden, this place is gorgeous."

"Thanks. I've always had a thing for log cabins, but I wanted a decent-sized house that had a bit more appeal than just four square walls."

"It sure has that," she exclaimed. "When I first met you, didn't you describe yourself as a cowboy who sells a few horses, and trains a few more?"

"That's who I am," he winked.

"You don't have a home like that selling a few horses, Caden."

"I didn't have to buy the land," he replied. "It was my dads, I just-"

"You just built a phenomenal house and created a super successful horse sales and training farm is what you did."

"With a little help from my friends, as Joe Cocker once said. You know who he is?"

"Yes, I do," she nodded. "You are a very impressive man, Caden Price."

"Jane must have found out about this place," he remarked. "That's probably the only reason she was so aggressive."

"I doubt it," Bridget murmured leaning across the console. "You are one sexy cowboy."

"Sit back in your seat please, young lady."

"Spoilsport," she quipped.

As he continued down a gravel road, two large barns came into view, and he rolled the van to a stop.

"Where is everyone?"

"Probably out checkin' fencin' or workin' some horses in the ring."

"Where's it, the ring I mean?"

"Over there," he replied pointing to a building that appeared to be an oversized barn.

"But, that's huge."

"We need huge. Remember, this is a trainin' and sales barn, and in the winter we can't stop 'cos there's snow on the ground."

"I can't wait to see it," she said excitedly.

"You look like your feelin' better," he remarked.

"Change of scenery maybe. I'm still hurting, but I'm so happy it's probably overriding not feeling good."

"Let's get your boy outta the van and into his paddock, then I have someone who's been waitin' to meet you."

It only took a few minutes to unload Valentino, and as he descended the ramp he whinnied loudly, his nose in the air and his ears pricked.

"They remember him," Bridget declared as the horses in the nearby paddocks whinnied their response.

"He was here for several weeks, and horses don't forget," Caden said as they began walking him towards a group of fenced paddocks.

"How many horses do you have?"

"We've got almost forty right now, all levels of trainin', many here to sell. There are five full-time handlers, and the maintenance workers.

It's not a small operation, but it's at the point where it kinda runs itself. I mean, everyone knows their job and they do it."

"What do you do?"

"Me? I sell. Correction, I ride and sell," he said stopping at one of the smaller paddocks. "He's gotta be in a pasture by himself for a few days, until I decide who to put him with him. The horses he was with before have been moved."

"Of course, I understand," Bridget replied as she removed his halter and watched her stunning chestnut dance and prance and become reacquainted with his friends. "This feels really good, being here with you."

"Yeah, it does. I knew it would," he smiled. "Come with me. Like I said, I have someone I want you to meet."

They walked across a wide driveway to the first of the two large barns, and entering the wide aisle, Bridget saw several horses poke their heads out over their stalls doors.

"These guys are in here 'cos they're bein' worked, or have just been worked, or they're still bein' evaluated," Caden explained.

"I've never seen a barn this big," Bridget declared.

"I don't leave my horses out in storms, they come in, and I have to have enough room. Here we are," he announced pulling open a stall door.

Moving beside him, Bridget peered inside and let out a low, soft whimper. A foal was moving around the oversized stall on spindly legs, his mother paying close attention.

"Ooh, Caden, she's absolutely adorable."

"Remember, you have to name her."

"I feel so honored."

"We'll start imprintin' soon. You know about that, of course."

"Yes, of course, you touch her and handle her and let her know we humans are good people."

"Yeah, basically," he chuckled.

"Wow. I'm totally blown away."

She stood staring, falling in love with the sweet, baby foal in front of her.

"Caden, if I name her, you know what that means, don't you?"

"Uh, maybe not. Tell me."

"You can never sell her. In fact, don't show me any foal you're going to raise and train and sell."

"Oh, Lord," he laughed. "We're gonna have a problem with that one. I'm real careful about who buys my horses, I promise."

"I believe you, but you can't sell this baby. Not if I name her."

"Then I guess you own two horses now," he grinned.

"No, I own Valentino, this girl belongs to us both," she decreed.

"Come here you gorgeous thing," he muttered pulling her into his arms, but as he did, he felt her wince and relaxed his hold.

"For the next few days the only thing you're gonna be doin' is gettin' healed up," he said firmly. "You need to be takin' it easy and lettin' your body mend itself, you hear me?"

"Yes, Caden, and you won't get any argument from me. Yesterday was a month rolled into a few hours, and all of a sudden I don't feel right."

"Let's get you up to the house and settle you in."

"That sounds good. I suppose it was because this morning was kind of hectic, but I'm feeling super tired. Strange, it's just come over me out of nowhere."

"There's a gator here. I'll zip us up in that and stop at the van to grab our bags on the way."

"Yes, please," she sighed. "I was feeling so good until few minutes ago."

"That'll probably happen, a burst of energy then you'll flag," he said closing the stall door. "The gator's right through here."

The trip up the drive was a short one, but as they stopped in front of the house, Caden could see Bridget was grateful for the lift. Picking up the bags he walked slowly up the steps beside her, and unlocking the front door he ushered her in.

"You're pale," he said looking down at her.

"Yeah, I'm feeling pale," she said quietly.

"You feel like you're gonna pass out, don't you?"

"Uh-huh."

Putting down the bags, and effortlessly lifting her into his arms, he carried her up the stairs, down a short hallway and into his bedroom, laying her on his king-sized bed.

"Sorry," she muttered.

"We should have waited a couple of days before doin' this," he grumbled. "My fault, I'm sorry, darlin'."

"Don't be sorry. I'm glad I'm here. It's so peaceful, and I'm not surrounded by drama and a ton of people."

"I'm gonna go make you some tea and get you somethin' to eat. Don't you move," he said shaking his finger at her.

"I couldn't even if I wanted to," she sighed, "which I don't."

"I'll be right back," he said softly.

He made his way down the stairs to the kitchen, and as he set the kettle to boil and popped some bread in the toaster, he thought about how happy he was to have her in his home.

"I'm gonna nurse you back to health, and I'm gonna take things real easy with you, but then, Bridget," he murmured, a grin crossing his lips, "I'm gonna open that special door, you're gonna walk down those stairs, and you're not gonna believe your eyes.

CHAPTER THIRTEEN

SHE WAS STANDING IN a red room. Everything was red. The walls, the bed, the lights. Different shades of red, but red. Staring down at her hands she was wearing red silk handcuffs. Wondering how there could be such a thing, she lifted her eyes, knowing Caden was in front of her and he would know the answer. Smiling down at her, he kissed her softly, touching her breast with a whisper of his finger.

"You're filled with passion you have yet to understand."

She was lost in his eyes, captivated by his words, and was about to ask a question when a strange buzzing sound rattled through the room. Frowning, deeply disturbed, she brought her hands to her ears. The handcuffs had disappeared, and suddenly her eyes blinked open. She had been ripped from a deep sleep, but the buzzing was still ringing in her ears, loud and insistent.

Cursing herself for not having left it on the nightstand, bleary-eyed she climbed from the bed, and stumbling across the room she picked it up from the desk.

Be here at ten ready to ride. Jane.

"That's weird," Bridget muttered. "Makes no sense. Huh. What's she up to?"

Staring across at the clock she saw it was nine-fifteen, and feeling slightly hung over, she moved into the bathroom to shower, but just as she was about to step under the water the phone rang. Turning off the faucets she raced back into the bedroom and snatched up the receiver.

"Hey, darlin.'"

"I knew it was you. How is everything?"

"Patty was so much better this mornin', and her baby, what a doll. I can't wait to introduce you. I want you to help me pick out a name."

"That would be fantastic. I would love that."

"Did you see Heather last night?"

"Caden, I did, and what a story," she exclaimed, "but it's something I have to tell you in person."

"What about this mornin'? I thought I'd be talkin' to you at the barn. Aren't you workin'?"

"That's another story, but one I'll tell you now. When Heather's mother called to arrange a lesson for Heather with me, Jane told her Heather had to be evaluated by her first, so she's riding with Jane at ten-thirty this morning. I just now got a page that she wants me there at ten, ready to get on."

"That's weird."

"Totally," Bridget declared. "I wish you were here. I don't like this. Not a bit."

"Go with the flow, darlin'. Don't react and don't provoke. I'll be leavin' here in about an hour."

"Can't you come sooner?"

"I'll try. I'm almost afraid not to. There won't be anyone there to keep the peace," he chuckled.

"I had the most wonderful dream about you, but it got interrupted. We where in this amazing red room."

"Red room?" he repeated.

"Yes, you said something very sexy to me, just not sure what it was now."

"You think about that dream if she tries to make you crazy."

"I will. I'd better run. I've just got time to get back to my cabin, grab some breakfast and change."

"See very soon, darlin'. Be good."

"I will. Drive carefully."

Hanging up the phone she hurried back to her shower. As the water washed away the last of her drowsiness, she told herself she'd stay calm and not react, but keep her wits. Something was wrong. She could feel it.

Dressing quickly, she trotted down the stairs, dashed through the kitchen and out the back door, but striding down the path to the cabins she slowed her step as she studied the sky. Thick, puffy clouds floated overhead, but in the distance she could see a forbidding, dark grey mass. It could skirt the ranch, or just as easy pummel them.

"I really hope your place isn't out there," she whispered. "Please get back soon."

Reaching her cabin she turned on the television, then changed into her favorite riding jeans and boots, and as she poured herself some granola she listened attentively to the morning news waiting for the weather forecast.

"Best get out your raincoats and umbrella's folks, we have a fast developing storm headed our way."

Picking up her cereal she carried it into the living room, and stood in front of the television eating as she watched. According to the forecaster the storm would pass directly over them in a couple of hours.

"Just when Caden will be arriving. I wonder if he knows. Shoot, I'm going to call him."

Reaching Celeste, she was able to get the phone number for his ranch, and to her relief he picked up on the first ring.

"I'm so glad I caught you," she said urgently. "There's a big storm, and it's supposed to be here-"

"Sorry to interrupt, darlin', but I just heard. I'm not hangin' around. I'm gonna help the boys bring in some horses, then I'm jumpin' in my car."

"Hurry, but still be careful."

"You bet."

Reassured, she dropped the bowl in her sink and headed up to the stable. As she walked into the barn aisle she saw Jane and Tim standing by the cross ties with two of the horses she'd been on the day before. They were both tacked up and ready to ride.

"Good morning."

"Hi, Bridget. Tim is going to take you out and show you our most popular trail."

"Now?"

"Yes, now," Jane said impatiently. "There'll be a storm here in a couple of hours, but you have enough time to do the loop."

Bridget was about to protest, then remembered Caden's advice and bit her tongue.

"Okay, great," she said. "I'd love to go out. Which horse do you want me to ride, or do you care?"

"Why don't you take Houston," Tim suggested. "Harley here is kinda my pal."

"Makes no difference to me," Bridget said walking past Jane and unhooking Houston from the cross ties. "Come on, fella, let's go have some fun."

From the corner of her eye Bridget saw Jane check her watch, but there was still almost twenty-five minutes before Heather was due. Something was up. Bridget had also noticed a mounting block in the stable yard, presumably for Heather.

Leading Houston out with Tim and Harley following, she climbed on board, walked away a few steps, then waited patiently for Tim to mount up.

"You ready?" Tim asked as he landed in his saddle.

"You bet. Where exactly will we be going?"

"We'll follow the trail to the meadow above the swimming hole, then turn left. It takes us up a small hill that bends around and drops us back on the other side of the barn. It's about forty-five minutes."

"Lead the way."

But a worried frown crinkled her brow. The barn and riding ring would be completely out of sight, and she had a strong feeling she should stay.

Tim started forward, and try as she might, Bridget couldn't think of a reason to get off her horse and stall. She started following him along the trail and into the trees, her concern growing. By the time they were approaching the meadow, her worry had turned into an over-whelming need to turn around and go back.

"Tim, hold up a minute."

"What? Is something wrong?" he asked pulling his horse to a stop.

"I'm going to be straight with you," she said solemnly.

"Okay, but why do I think I'm not going to like this?"

"It's painfully obvious that the only reason we're out here is because Jane wants me away from the barn."

"Yeah, I figured that when I got the page this mornin'."

"I'm going back. I'll cut around the far side of the barn so she won't see me, but I have to find out what it is she doesn't want me to know about."

"You realize you could lose your job, right?"

"I don't care, I really don't, besides, with her in charge I'm only go-ing to last five minutes anyway."

"I think I know what she's doin'," Tim said slowly. "I'm kinda sur-prised you haven't cottoned-on."

"What?"

"The only reason I could think of, is that she wants to ride Valenti-no."

"Shit. Of course. I'm an idiot. Thanks, Tim. I'm outta here."

Turning Houston around she broke into a canter, continuing on until she reached the middle of the wooded area, then slowed to a walk. Moving behind the barn she skirted around the long side, and ap-proached the stable yard just in time to see Jane leading Valentino up to the mounting block. Kicking Houston into a fast trot she burst forward, and jumping from the saddle, flipped the reins over the horses head and marched up to her.

"What the hell?" Jane shouted staring at her in shock.

"I could say the same thing to you," Bridget shouted back. "Caden told you, that horse is not to be ridden by anyone but me."

"Too bad. The client wants to ride him, and at this ranch we give the client what they want. That means I have to ride him first."

"The hell you will," Bridget exclaimed.

The sound of the golf cart caught Bridget's attention, and turning around she saw Heather and her mother rolling towards them. Her heart sank. Celeste wasn't with them. Celeste was a smart, reasonable woman, and Bridget was sure she would have read the situation correctly and stepped in. The cart rolled to a stop, and Molly climbed out and marched forward.

"Thank you for arranging this, Jane. It's nice to meet you."

"You too, Mrs. Chadwick. I think you'll find Valentino here to be everything I told you, and more."

"From what I saw from the terrace yesterday, I believe he'll be just perfect. I'm looking forward to seeing him go with you on board."

"Uh, what exactly is going on here?" Bridget asked.

"Heather likes this horse," Molly replied impatiently, "so Jane is going to give us a demonstration, and then give her a lesson on him. What's it to you?"

"I'm sorry, but this horse is not for a beginner," Bridget said politely, wondering why the woman was being so rude.

"My daughter is not a beginner," Molly snapped, "and Jane is the person in charge here. She's made it clear you're just one of the stable hands. You shouldn't be interfering with matters that don't concern you."

"Mother, please. I haven't ridden in a western saddle," Heather interjected.

Bridget was about to point out that the horse didn't belong to the ranch, when a movement caught her eye, and turning around she saw Jane had reached the top step of the mounting block and was about to get on.

"Jane, do not get on that horse!"

"You have zero authority here," she barked. "What you say is irrelevant."

Bridget had no thought as she exploded into action. Throwing Houston's reins at a startled Heather, she lunged forward, shoving Jane off the mounting block sending her tumbling to the ground. Leaping to the top step in a single bound, she climbed quickly into the saddle, and with a cluck and a kick she was cantering across the stable yard.

"My heavens," Molly exclaimed running across to Jane. "Are you all right?"

"That girl's insane," Jane muttered as she got to her feet, "and she's now unemployed."

Heather had kept Bridget and Valentino in her sights, and watched them gallop around the outside of the arena and start up a hill, covering the ground with remarkable speed. "I'm reporting her to Richard Tate," she heard her mother bark. "I'm going up to the office right now."

"That's not necessary," Jane said quickly. "Please, Mrs. Chadwick, I need to handle this personally. I'll fetch another horse for Heather to ride."

Hearing her name, Heather was about to turn around when she saw the big chestnut in the distance disappear over the hill.

"I'll put her on Lilly," Jane continued. "She's a very sweet mare."

"Uh, no, that's okay," Heather said pulling her eyes away and leading Houston forward. "I'm not really in the mood now."

"Heather, let's not be hasty," Molly said quickly. "Riding is good for you."

"No, mother, not today," Heather replied handing Houston's reins to Jane. "I'm going back to the house. If you want to stay here, I'll walk up and leave you the golf cart."

"No, no, I'm coming. I'm very sorry, Jane. Thank you for all your efforts. I do appreciate them."

"You're welcome, Mrs. Chadwick, and don't worry, I'll sort this out."

Already sitting behind the wheel, Heather waited impatiently as Molly climbed in.

"I don't know what's wrong with you," Molly muttered as Heather headed up the driveway. "You could have had a lesson on another horse."

"It wasn't about the horse, Mother, it was about Jane."

"It seems to me that other girl, that Bridget, she's the one with the problem."

"You have no idea what you're talking about."

"Don't I just? I've been around-"

"The block more times than you, my girl," Heather interrupted. "I've heard that ten thousand times, and I'm sick of it."

"Heather. How dare you speak to me like that!"

"I need some peace," Heather snapped pulling up to the front door. "Please don't bother me for a while. I'm getting a headache."

"Do you want some Aleve, or-"

"No, mother, I just want to be left alone," she said tersely. "I'll call you later."

Stepping from the cart Heather hurried inside, ran up the stairs and into her room. Locking the door, she took a deep breath, walked into the bedroom, sat on the bed, and picking the phone she dialed Jeff's number.

BACK AT THE BARN JANE was seriously irritated. She'd virtually sold Valentino to the Chadwick woman over the phone, and for a highly inflated price, a price she was sure Caden would not have been able to turn down.

"Who else can I sell to that stupid woman? Still, it wasn't a complete loss," she muttered as she put Houston into a stall. "In fact, I think it's going to work out very well indeed."

The sound of a horse in the yard made her pause, and moving quickly down the barn aisle, stepping outside she found Tim climbing off Harley.

"Where the hell have you been, and what made Bridget turn around and come back here?"

"I don't know, Jane," he said calmly, leading his horse into the barn.

"What do you mean, you don't know?" Jane demanded as she followed him.

"I turned around and she was gone," Tim lied. "I rode around for a bit looking for her. I thought maybe she'd fallen off or something, and I'd missed it."

"Fuck."

Ignoring her outburst, Tim placed his horse in the cross ties and began unsaddling him, watching Jane from the corner of his eye.

"Don't you even want to know what happened?" she asked staring at him. "You're always so, so, so, controlled. So, uninterested, or what, bored?"

"Just don't wanna poke my nose in, or cause any problems," he replied, then casually added, "I am curious about one thing though."

"You are?" she exclaimed. "I can't believe it."

"I don't think you like your job very much, and I-"

"What's to like?" she snapped interrupting him.

"I've often wondered why you stay here?" he continued, his voice even and measured.

"Why do you think? To nail a rich bastard, of course. Where else am I going to meet wealthy men. I almost got one a couple of months ago, but his wife's radar must have gone off because they left in a big hurry. Sonofabitch didn't even say goodbye."

"That explains it then," Tim said brushing his horse. "Did Bridget go home?"

"She took off on Valentino," Jane snapped.

"Valentino? I don't understand."

"She came back and attacked me. I was showing Valentino to Heather Chadwick and her mother and Bridget went nuts. She pushed me off the mounting block and jumped on."

"She did? That's intense," Tim remarked. *Good for you Bridget.*

"She went off towards the hills on the other side of the arena."

"She did? That's not a great area to be riding alone," Tim frowned.

"That's her problem. I don't give a shit. Hurry up. I'm going to find the grooms and start bringing the horses in for the storm. We've got to fill their water buckets and pull their blankets out."

"Sure. I'll just pick out Harely's feet and put him away," Tim replied, but if Bridget didn't return soon, he'd be off to look for her.

A SHORT TIME LATER, zipping down the interstate, keeping his eyes peeled for the highway patrol, Caden was nearing the turnoff. His crew didn't want him driving in the approaching storm, so they'd refused to let him help bring in the horses. Knowing they had plenty of time, and grateful for the opportunity to get away quickly, he'd jumped in his car and sped off.

As he exited the freeway and drove down the road that would take him to Dudley's, he thought about stopping at the local florist and buying Bridget some flowers, but in a hurry to get back to her, he changed his mind. The road was empty as he continued on, and heading up the gentle hill he entered the picturesque driveway, pulled the car around to the back of the large house and into the garage. Walking inside he moved down the hallway into the foyer, and was about to head up the stairs when he was stopped by a flustered Celeste.

"Caden," she said nervously, "we have a problem."

"What kind of problem."

"At the barn, with Bridget."

An icy hand wrapped around his heart and began to squeeze.

"Go on," he said trying to control his fear.

"From what I understand, Jane was trying to ride Valentino. Apparently she'd promised Heather Chadwick a lesson on him."

"What?"

"Bridget pushed her off the mounting block and climbed on Valentino herself. She galloped away and uh, well, she hasn't come back."

"How long ago was this?"

"Oh, probably, thirty minutes, maybe forty. We're worried about the storm, and, uh, she went over the east hills."

"Damn. Call the barn for me and ask them to tack up Goliath. I'm gonna go find her. Is the golf cart out front?"

"Yes, Caden. Good luck."

Running outside he jumped into the cart and raced down to the barn.

"Bridget, where are you?" he muttered. "Why haven't you come back? Please, be safe, please, please, please."

CHAPTER FOURTEEN

WHEN CADEN REACHED the stable yard and climbed from the golf cart, he was met by the start of a soft drizzle. Entering the barn he discovered Tim standing with Goliath in the cross ties already tacked up.

"That was fast," Caden remarked.

"I was just about to go and look for her myself," Tim said urgently. "I'm worried."

"Were you here when she took off?" Caden asked as he ducked into the tack room to search out a parka.

"I saw everything," Tim replied following him in. "There's a goose-down waterproof jacket in that end cabinet that should fit her, and a man's mac hanging in that steel closet."

Donning the raincoat first, he opened the cabinet, and pulling out the down parka he rolled it into a ball.

"Put this in the saddle bag for me," he said handing it off to Tim. "Where's the first aid kit?"

"Top cabinet on the right," Tim called over his shoulder.

Finding the small canvas bag, Caden hurried it back to the cross ties, handing it off to Tim to add to the parka.

"I'd like to come with you."

"Thanks, but I need you to stay here in case she comes back," Caden replied as he snatched a lead rope and halter, looping it around the saddle horn.

"I don't know the range of the pagers," Tim said anxiously, "but when you find her, if she's still wearin' hers-"

"If she is I'll start pagin' you as I head back," Caden interrupted leading Goliath out of the cross ties. "We'll come within range at some point."

"Good luck, be careful," Tim said anxiously as he followed Caden outside and watched him mount up.

Caden trotted out of the stable yard, then broke into a canter as he passed the arena and headed towards the east hills. As he neared the base of the gentle slope, the misty drizzle became a light rain, and he knew the tumult of the storm wasn't far behind. He also knew that out of all the horses on the property, Goliath was the one to be on. Part draft horse, he was a cool customer and virtually bomb proof.

The trail up the hill offered separate branches. One looped around a thicket of trees and dropped back down on the opposite side of the arena. It was a quick ride, thirty minutes at a leisurely pace.

The second took the rider to the very top of the hill. The last part was steep and not for the faint of heart, but the views were spectacular. The only way down was to follow the trail back, and if Bridget had chosen that path and was somewhere near the top, it would be a frightening and dangerous ride bringing her down the steep slope in the wet conditions.

The third was the least desirable of the three. The trail wound down into a rocky canyon. It was rarely ridden because continuous rock slides would block the path, and there were several places where the trail became extremely narrow.

As Caden started up the hill the rain picked up, and he pulled the hood of the slicker over his head. Goliath was undaunted as he clambered forward, and it seemed to Caden the horse was enjoying his trek out in the rain. His ears were pricked and there was plenty of energy in his step. The minutes ticked by, and through the rain Caden saw the area where he could turn off and start down the trail into the rocky canyon. Convinced she wouldn't have taken the route, they passed it by, but as they continued up the hill, to Caden's dismay the rain grew stronger. The fearless horse, however, unflinchingly continued forward, and when a roll of thunder announced the storm's dark presence, true to his nature, Goliath wasn't fazed. Caden, though, felt his pulse tick up, and as they reached the turn off that would loop around past the trees and take them back down, he pulled the big horse to a halt. He could continue up the hill to the top, or veer off towards the trees and home.

His mind raced.

If she was on the steep part of the trail near the top he wouldn't be able to see her in the heavy weather. She'd been aware the storm was on its way, but she'd never been on the trail, and wouldn't know how steep it became. She also wouldn't know the one to the left would take her home, or would she? She'd done a ton of trail riding and had great instincts.

Unexpectedly Goliath made the decision for him, abruptly turning and marching off down the trail to the left, towards the thicket of trees.

"I hope you know somethin' I don't," Caden muttered. "Please, Lord, you spared my mare and new foal, please make it a triple and lead me to my beautiful Bridget."

The trail was cut into the side of the hill, level and fairly wide, and though it had been there for many years, Caden hugged the inside of the track. The rain was pounding and he was worried the edge might give way under Goliath's heavy hooves. It seemed to be taking forever to reach the shelter of the thicket and there was still no sign of her, but the trees were dense, and he continued to pray fervently that Bridget was somewhere inside, that she'd taken her time to explore, and then stayed there when the rain had started.

"Please, dear God, please, please," he mumbled reaching the boundary of the trees.

The trail went around the thicket, not through it, but he'd ridden it once before and had found his way under the trees to the other side. He was trying to decide which way to go, when once again Goliath made the choice, turning off the trail and moving under the thick canopy of heavy green branches.

"I sure hope you know where you're takin' me," he said patting the horse's soaked neck.

Caden was surprised by the amount of shelter the trees provided, and immensely grateful for the temporary relief, but they'd only walked a short distance when Goliath abruptly stopped, pricked his ears, and lifted his head. Caden stopped breathing, listening intently, but all he could hear was the sound of the rain hitting the leaves. He closed his leg, asking Goliath to move on, but the big horse wouldn't budge, then unexpectedly he let out a loud whinny. Seconds later, Caden heard a whinny in response.

"Valentino! Holy crap, Goliath, you've found them!"

Without being asked Goliath started forward, walking briskly through the trees, continuing to call to his friend, each call being returned. Caden's heart was racing as the horse carried him through the dense thicket, then suddenly, Valentino was standing directly in front of him, standing stock still. He stared at them for a second, then dropped his head to the ground. Caden looked down at the carpet of thick leaves, and to his relief, then fear, he saw Bridget's limp body. Jumping from the saddle he raced forward, and kneeling beside her he gently rolled her on to her back and moved the wet hair off her face.

"Bridget, Bridget, wake up," he begged staring at the multitude of scratches across her right cheek.

She could hear him. It was Caden. She was swimming in a lake, but it was cold. She wanted to get out, but she couldn't find her way back to shore.

"Caden," she breathed. "Help me."

Caden's heart skipped many beats, and fighting back the tears he sat her up and pulled her into his body.

"Bridget, thank you, thank you."

Goliath was only a few steps away, and looking up he saw both horses were completely focused on him. He could feel their energy. They were in this together, all three of them. Gently resting Bridget against a tree, Caden hurried to his saddle bag and pulled out the parka. She was cold and wet, but he knew the goose down would help the chill, and as he slid the puffy jacket up her arms and zipped it closed, her eyelids fluttered open.

"Caden?"

"Thank, God," he muttered. "Hey, darlin'."

"What happened?"

"You must have fallen off," he said quietly.

"No, no, I didn't, did I?"

"Does anything hurt? Can you stand up?"

"My whole body hurts, and I'm really cold."

"Are you dizzy?"

"Uh, no, just kind of, fuzzy."

"Try and stand. Put your arms around my neck."

Leaning against him, she managed to rise to her feet.

"How's that?" he asked studying her eyes.

"I remember now. I got off, I'm not sure why, then I tripped some-how. I remember hitting my head and stinging pain down the side of my face."

"Thank God I found you," he mumbled feeling her tremble against him.

"You're here," she frowned.

"Yes, darlin', I'm here, and I'm gonna pony you back down."

"You don't need to pony me," she mumbled.

"Uh, yes, I do," he smiled, grateful that she had the wherewithal to argue. "Come on, walk for a minute, make sure you're not dizzy."

"No, I'm not dizzy, I just feel sore, and the side of my face hurts."

"It's a bit scratched up," he murmured, slowly walking her back and forth. "Do you still have your pager?"

"Um, my pager, uh, yes, here," she said unsnapping it from her belt. "Please, take me back now."

"Let's get your head covered first," he said.

Taking the pager from her, he pulled the parka's hood over her head and tied it under her chin. "There you go. It's pouring."

"It's not so bad," she replied feeling a shiver.

"We're under the trees. Once we're out of here there's no shelter."

"Will you help me on to Valentino?"

"I'm thinking you should sit behind me on Goliath."

"No, it's better for me to sit on Valentino, honestly. I want to."

"I think you'd be better off holding on to me."

"No, please, I hate riding like that. I need to sit on Valentino," she repeated.

He paused, looking around and spotted a sawn off tree trunk.

"There," he said, "a mounting block."

"Yes, good, I can just climb on," she muttered.

Leading Valentino across to the stump, Caden held him steady as Bridget slowly clambered on to the flat top, and as she slowly stood up, steadying herself by holding on to the saddle, he changed his mind.

"No, you're not all right," he declared. "You need to sit behind me on Goliath."

"I'm okay," she groaned, and before he could stop her she'd put her foot in the stirrup, swung her leg over, and was sitting in the saddle. "See?"

"Damn, you're stubborn," he grumbled.

"Please take me home," she repeated. "Seriously."

Muttering under his breath, cursing himself for not having put her on Goliath, he retrieved the halter and lead rope from the saddle horn and slipped it over Valentino's bridle. Moments later he was mounted up, the lead rope in his hand, and Valentino next to him.

"Are you ready?" he asked staring at her white face. "Are you sure you don't wanna just slip on Goliath behind me?"

"No, honestly. This is better."

"If you have any problems, you tell me right away."

"I will," she nodded.

Not sure how to find his way out of the woods, Caden told Goliath to move ahead, then just left him alone. The big brave horse had led him to Bridget, and he had full confidence that Goliath would find his way home. He was right. As though he'd done it a hundred times before, Goliath walked a direct path to the edge of the thicket and out into the rain.

"I would never have seen that exit," he mumbled as he turned to make sure Bridget was all right. "Thank you, Goliath."

The rain was a downpour, and as they made their way slowly down the hill, Caden dropped the reins and paged Tim.

Found Bridget. Coming down west side of hill. Have car and blankets waiting. Confirm.

He waited for the response, and when it came through he let out a heavy breath. They'd soon be back at the barn, he'd put Bridget in the car, then whisk her into a hot bath.

The worst of the storm was almost upon them, and when they hit flat ground, as much as he wanted to hasten their step, not trusting Bridget's balance he kept them at a walk. He knew it was too muddy for a car to reach them, and he'd have to pass the arena before they'd hit gravel, but then he saw it; the black Range Rover was driving through the mud..

Halting the horses he slipped out of his saddle, and just as the Range Rover pulled up, a massive clap of thunder burst over their heads. Goliath didn't move, but Valentino began shifting his feet. Talking calmly he managed to settle the horse's nerves, and glancing back at the SUV, he saw Tim running towards them. Helping Bridget off, he kept her in his arms ready to carry her to the car.

"I'll take the horses," Tim shouted, and taking hold of Valentino's lead rope, he climbed aboard Goliath.

Carrying Bridget to the Rover, Caden saw Richard climbing from the driver's seat to open the back door. Settling her inside, Caden pulled off the drenched parka and wrapped her in the dry, warm blankets waiting on the back seat.

"How is she?" Richard asked as he maneuvered the car through the mud.

"A bit banged up, but okay I think," Caden replied.

"I'm all right," she quivered.

"I've called a doctor," Richard said. "He's on his way."

"First thing I'm gonna do is put her in a hot bath," Caden declared.

"Yes, please," she bleated as another chill shivered through her.

"Thank God you found her," Richard said gravely.

"It was Goliath who found her," Caden remarked snuggling her against him.

"Horses. I've never understood them," Richard said. "I've always been a bit scared of them if I'm honest. Crazy that I ended up having a luxury dude ranch. It really was Goliath who found her?"

"Yep, took me directly to her in the middle of that thicket of trees on the side of the hill."

"He did?" Bridget squeaked.

"He did, darlin', and Valentino was standin' right over you."

"Really?"

"Really, like he was watching out for you, like a guardian angel."

"Okay, we're here," Richard announced stopping under the portico at the front door of the house. "I'll call your room when the doctor arrives."

"Thanks, Richard," Caden said gratefully, and lifting Bridget out of the car, he carried her inside, up to their suite, and walking directly into the bedroom, he sat her on the edge of the bed.

"Stay in those blankets," he said firmly, and walking into the bathroom, he turned on the faucets and dropped some lavender bath gel into the tub.

"I'm sorry," she said softly.

Turning around he saw her standing in the doorway.

"Don't you do anything you're told?" he asked walking over to her.

"I couldn't sit there," she mumbled. "Please hold me."

"Darlin'," he sighed wrapping her up in his arms, "I didn't mean to scold. I've been sick with worry."

"I'm sorry," she repeated. "I was going to stay on the side of the hill until I figured I'd be gone long enough for you to get back, but..."

"But then things went wrong."

"Yes," she nodded, "things went wrong."

"Let's get you undressed, then I'm going to order you up some hot soup."

"Tea as well, please. The British blend."

"You must be feelin' better," he smiled as he began removing the blankets.

"Kind of, except I feel all shaky."

"The bath will help," he promised.

"Caden?"

"Yes, darlin'?"

"When I felt myself passing out, I knew you were coming to help me. The feeling was so strong."

"I'll always come for you," he said softly, peeling off the last of her clothes. "Now let's get your butt in that hot water."

Holding her steady as she stepped into the bath, he watched her sink into the aromatic, relaxing foam.

"You soak. I'm gonna call downstairs for that soup, then check in with Tim. If you need me just call and I'll come runnin.'"

"Okay," she sighed closing her eyes. "You're my hero."

Stepping back into the bedroom, he called down to the kitchen and placed his food order, then rang the barn.

"Tim Colson."

"Tim, it's Caden. How are the horses?"

"We toweled them off real well, then put on their blankets and put them in their stalls. They seem fine, both eatin' real good."

"Thanks, Tim. I know Richard will want to talk to you, and I do as well. I want to know exactly what happened."

"I've already talked to Richard and I'm meetin' up with him in a little while. If you're not busy, you should join us if you can."

"Good suggestion. I will, but one quick question."

"Go ahead."

"Did Bridget overreact?"

"Hmm, well, she was in an impossible situation. If she hadn't done what she did and let Jane do whatever she'd wanted, Heather Chadwick would probably have ended up tryin' to ride a horse that was too much for her, and we all know how that can end."

"Thanks, Tim. I'll talk to you later."

Finally able to pull off his own soaked clothes, Caden began to undress.

"I'll take a shower after the doc has come and gone," he mumbled under his breath. "If there's one way to put someone in touch with their heart, it's drama. I knew I loved you, Bridget, but I didn't realize how much. Screw the flowers. I know exactly what I'm gonna give you."

CHAPTER FIFTEEN

THE KITCHEN SENT UP a bowl of tomato-basil soup and a grilled cheese sandwich for them both, along with a pot of tea and a carafe of coffee. Bridget devoured both the sandwich and soup, washing down her meal with two cups of tea. The storm had caused a problem with the roads, but the doctor finally arrived, and after a thorough check-up Bridget was told she'd suffered no concussion. There were, however, many scrapes and abrasions that needed tending, especially on her hands and the side of her face.

Caden sat quietly as the doctor set about his work, deeply disturbed by the entire incident. Jane's arrogance was beyond measure. If what Tim told him was true, he didn't blame Bridget one bit for what she'd done, but he still had questions.

"There you are, young lady," the doctor said rising from the side of the bed. "All your wounds are superficial, but they're going to be sore for the next few days. Make sure you keep them clean and dry. You should change the bandages in forty-eight hours. Aspirin or ibuprofen as you need it."

"Thanks so much, Doctor," she murmured. "I feel a bit strange."

"You've been through a trauma and you need to rest. Tomorrow you'll probably find some new aches and pains, but that strange feeling should be gone."

Caden walked him to the door, thanking him profusely for driving through the storm.

"I'm just glad there was nothing serious. She must have rolled over some branches. All those abrasions wouldn't have come from a simple fall."

"That occurred to me as I watched you patch her up and saw the extent of them," Caden agreed.

"Make sure she gets plenty of rest."

"I will. It's still nasty out there. Maybe you should stick around until it lets up a bit. They have wonderful coffee and desserts here. Please, order what you want and put it on my tab."

"That's not necessary," the doctor smiled, "but thank you for the offer, though I just might have a little something before I hit the road."

Closing the door behind him, Caden moved across and sat on the bed, staring at the many scrapes across the side of her face.

"How did you get so many scratches, darlin'?"

"I don't remember."

"You say you got off for some reason, do you remember what that reason was? Do you know why you went into the woods?"

"Why did I go into the woods? Let me think. I remember finding the trail that would loop me around. I'd seen it from the arena."

"Ah, I thought you might have."

"I started down. It was cold, and it was starting to rain. I remember thinking the storm would be on me soon, and then...something happened. Darn it, I can't picture it."

"It'll come back to you," Caden said reassuringly. "I think it's time you got some rest. I'm gonna jump in the shower real quick, then go down and to talk to Richard."

"Caden, are you mad at me?"

"No, darlin', no, of course not. Tim told me what happened. He saw the whole thing, I am curious though, why you didn't just ride into the arena. Why did you head up into the hills?"

"That's what I wanted to do, go into the ring, but when I got close I saw the gate was closed and I was afraid to get off."

"Because you were worried Jane would come runnin' up and you'd get into another scene."

"Exactly, so I went up to the other end, but that gate had a chain and a padlock around it. That's when I figured I'd just ride up the hill and come back around. What about Jane? Have you seen her? She's such a horrible person. How could she be working here? I don't understand it."

"That's what I intend to find out," Caden frowned. "I'm gonna go take that shower and you need to go to bed."

"I don't need to be told twice," she yawned slowly standing up. "Wow, listen to that rain."

"It's a helluva storm," Caden remarked, and putting his arm around her, he walked with her into the bedroom, took off her robe, and helped her into bed.

"I have to tell you about Heather and Jeff Ludlow," she yawned.

"It can wait," he said pulling the bedcovers over her.

"I think her mother drugged Jeff, sprawled him out on a hotel bed, then had his picture taken with a half-naked woman and sent it anonymously to Bridget."

"Unbelievable," Caden muttered.

"I told you it was a story," she said yawning again. "I don't know if I'm right yet. Heather was going to call Jeff today, but I haven't talked to her, uh, obviously."

"That's enough now," Caden said firmly. "Get to sleep. That's an order."

"Yes, Sir."

Closing her eyes, Bridget felt the heavy fatigue move through her body. Her knee was hurting, as were the cuts on her hands and face, but they didn't prevent her from drifting into sleep. The last thought that floated through her mind was Caden, and how grateful she was that he'd found his way back into her life.

Stepping into the bedroom after his shower, Caden found her already asleep, and quietly dressing, he tiptoed from the room and softly closed the door. Standing at the living room window, he stared out at the tumult. The wind was whipping the trees, the rain was pounding, and he decided to make a quick call to his ranch before heading off to talk to Richard.

"Everything's fine here, Caden," his foreman said. "Crazy ass storm though."

"How's Patty and the foal?"

"No problems. Glad you got back safe. We've been hopin' you'd call."

"Better check all the fencin' once this thing passes."

"Yep, we will. You relax, everything here is under control."

Hanging up the phone, Caden felt a new appreciation for his crew. Most of them had been with him for several years, and each of them was an outstanding horseman, and as honest as any man could be.

"How the hell did a woman like Jane end up workin' for Richard?" he muttered. "I've gotta get to the bottom of this."

Walking briskly out the door, he headed down the stairs and turned down the hallway, but as he passed Celeste's office, he saw her door was open so he poked his head around. She was on the phone, but signaled for him to sit down.

"Yes, Mrs. Chadwick, I'll have your bill sent up first thing in the morning. Yes, the Range Rover will be outside waiting at ten. You're welcome, and we're sorry you're leaving us prematurely. Yes, Mrs. Chadwick, goodbye."

"Heather and her mother are leavin'?" Caden asked. "They just got here."

"Not Heather and her mother, just her mother," Celeste answered. "Close the door."

Intrigued, Caden shut the door, and quickly returned to his seat.

"How's Bridget?" Celeste asked. "I've been concerned, though I ran into Doctor Peters and he said she'd be fine."

"She will be, but she's got cuts all over her hands and face," Caden replied, "and she can't remember what happened."

"Huh, well, it will come to her, I'm sure. Give it time."

"What were you going to tell me about the Chadwicks?"

"Oh, yes. Just before Mrs. Chadwick called to say she was leaving, you'll never guess who called to say he'd be arriving tomorrow."

"Jeff Ludlow," Caden said with a wide grin.

"Jeff Ludlow," Celeste repeated, "and he said he didn't care if he had to sleep in a tent, he wanted a reservation."

"Let me guess. You're givin' him Mrs. Chadwick's suite. How's that for irony?"

"Amazing, huh? I'd love to know what that's all about," she said rolling her eyes.

"Things have a way of gettin', out," Caden grinned. "I'm sure you'll know soon enough. Do you know if Richard is in his office?"

"He is, and he's asked me to join him for a meeting with Tim."

"I need to be there too. It's about what happened with Bridget, but I have some questions about Jane outside of this whole fiasco."

"He wants to find out exactly what happened," Celeste said, "and talk to Tim about the barn in general."

"Let's go in then," Caden said rising to his feet.

Walking the short distance to Richard's office, they knocked and entered, and discovered Tim was already there.

"Caden, I was just about to track you down. Celeste, good, please sit down. All right Tim, we're all here. Please tell us exactly what happened this morning."

"I don't need to," he replied reaching into his pocket and retrieving his phone. "I recorded the whole thing."

Starting the video for the very surprised trio, he placed his phone on Richard's desk, and they leaned in to watch the event unfold. When it reached the point where Bridget rode away, Celeste and Richard sat back to consider the drama they'd just seen and heard. Caden, though, kept watching, and as the video continued, he caught something else.

"You need to hear this bit comin' up," Tim declared interrupting his thoughts. "My phone was sittin' on the shelf so there's nothin' to see, but the audio is all you need."

There was a blip, then a fresh recording started, replaying Tim's conversation with Jane inside the barn.

"I've often wondered why you stay here."

"Why do you think? To nail a rich bastard, of course. Where else am I going to meet wealthy men. I almost got one a couple of months ago, but his wife's radar must have gone off because they left in a big hurry. Sonofabitch didn't even say goodbye."

"Turn it off," Richard growled.

"Over the last few months I've been recordin' her," Tim admitted. "I knew it was only a matter of time before she went too far, and I wanted to make sure I had it on video so if you needed it, you'd have it."

"Why didn't you come to me sooner?" Richard asked.

"Most of what she did was minor stuff, and I'm just a worker bee. I really love my job, Richard, and I didn't wanna risk losin' it by comin' forward too soon, or bein' seen as a complainer."

"Jane called me this morning," Richard said shaking his head, "and her version of events is vastly different from what you captured on video. That was smart, Tim, very smart, and I'm grateful."

"You're welcome. You can keep that and download everything on there. I only have stuff with Jane, so feel free. If you don't need me for anything else, I should get back to the horses. They were all calm when I left, but with the thunder still rollin', I'd feel better if I was there."

"Yes, you go, and Tim, thank you. Good work."

Caden remained quiet as Tim left the room, then looked across at Richard, waiting for him to speak.

"I'm astounded," Richard muttered. "That girl has been here for almost a year. Never had a single complaint."

"Richard, I owe you an apology," Caden said quietly.

"You? Why?"

"A few months back, Jane literally, physically, threw herself at me. It was surprising, to say the least, and I should have mentioned it."

"I probably would have brushed it off," Richard frowned. "You're not an unattractive man, Caden. I'm sure you've had other women make their uh, wishes, known."

"Not like this," Caden said raising his eyebrows.

"I have some other, extremely unfortunate news," Richard said with a heavy frown. "Not something I wanted to discuss in front of Tim."

"Oh, no, now what?" Celeste asked with a worried frown.

"When Jane called me this morning, she informed me she plans to sue me, and Bridget."

"Richard!" Celeste exclaimed. "No! You take such wonderful care of everyone here, that's, that's..."

"Extremely disturbing," Richard grimaced.

"Richard," Caden said slowly, "where did you find her? How did she come to work for you?"

"Max. Max hired her, but Max has been with me for over five years, you know that, and Max is solid, isn't he?"

"Max is still a man," Caden sighed, "and Jane is a very conniving, manipulative female."

"I don't even know what to say," Richard said heavily. "Obviously Jane is leaving immediately, which means I have only Max and Tim to deal with a full calendar coming up. Do I have to worry about Max?"

"I suspect, if Max did allow himself to be, shall we say, a bit corrupted, he's probably learned his lesson," Caden remarked. "I've always liked Max. He knows his stuff."

"If I may," Celeste said raising her hand.

"Please," Richard said rubbing his temples.

"Putting Jane and the threat of her lawsuit aside for a minute, Caden, how would you feel about finding us a new handler?"

"Uh, sure. Off the top of my head I know a couple of people that would probably be real happy to have a job here."

"If Caden brings someone in, Max won't have a stake in it. He'll be removed, if you see what I mean," Celeste continued.

"Yes, Celeste, I do see what you mean," Richard nodded. "If you're willing, Caden, I'd be very grateful."

"Yep, no problem, happy to help," Caden replied.

"About Tim," Celeste continued. "Might I suggest that he has earned the right to be promoted?"

"He's a quiet young man. I've never thought of him as a managerial type," Richard said thoughtfully.

"Quiet and calm is a good trait to have around horses," Caden said wisely, "and that sort of energy permeates the barn. With Max overseein' him, I think he can do the job."

"When it comes to barns and horses, Caden, I trust your judgement completely. You're batting a thousand so far, Celeste. What else have you got?"

"Thank you, Richard. I do have one more suggestion. I don't know how Bridget feels about staying on, but if she plans to leave, ask her if she will wait until Caden finds us a replacement for her. Those are my suggestions," Celeste finished.

"Caden, what about Bridget?" Richard asked.

"With Jane gone, I'm sure she'd be happy to stick around."

"My goodness, I came into this meeting with nothing but problems and questions, and it's ending with solutions and answers," Richard declared. "Except for Jane and her threat of a lawsuit of course," he added soberly. "See, Caden, see why Celeste must never leave my side?"

"I do," Caden chuckled. "I think this is a good time to ask for a raise, Celeste."

"Granted, whatever it is," Richard exclaimed.

"I'll have to give that some thought," Celeste smiled as she rose from her chair. "I have some arrangements to make. We have a new, last minute guest. I can pause for five minutes to solve the world's problems, but now I must continue with my work."

"Someone new, or a regular?" Richard inquired.

"New, Jeff Ludlow."

"Ah, a romance is about to renew itself?"

"I think that's a possibility," Celeste smiled as she headed to the door.

"Have a bottle of chilled champagne waiting for him, and some of those chocolate dipped strawberries and cream."

"My thoughts exactly," Celeste replied moving to the door.

They watched her leave, then Caden turned back to Richard.

"About Bridget, I don't know what her plans are, but I'm sure I can get you someone new pretty quick if she does want to move on. I do have a request though."

"What's that?"

"I want Bridget to myself for two days at my ranch the minute she's feelin' better. I can have one of my guys fill in."

"How can I say no?" Richard smiled.

"Thanks. In a way, Richard, you kinda owe that girl."

"I realize that," Richard nodded. "If she hadn't be so protective of that horse, she would never have challenged Jane the way she did, and I'd still be sitting here with my thumb up my ass."

"Richard! I've never heard you talk that way," Caden chuckled.

"Hey, it's how I'm feeling right now. Sometimes there are only certain phrases that adequately describe a situation. I can't repeat what I'm thinking about Jane's lawsuit though."

"You leave that to me," Caden said standing up. "Which is her cottage?"

"Caden, you must tread carefully with someone who has litigation on their mind."

"Richard, you said you trust my judgement with horses and barns?"

"Yes, absolutely, one-thousand percent."

"I have the same judgement when it comes to women, at least, most of the time," he added with a grin. "I can work this out for you."

"I'll be holding my breath until I hear from you!"

"It won't take long," Caden promised. "Listen to the rest of what Tim recorded. It'll be a distraction until I get back."

"I'm almost afraid to," Richard sighed staring at the phone on his desk.

"I doubt it could be much worse than what you've already heard."

"You're probably right. Good luck with Jane."

"If anyone needs luck it's her, but I think her luck just ran out. Which is her cottage?"

"It's the largest one, grey and white, closest to the east paddock, sort of set off by itself."

"Back soon. Keep the faith."

Leaving the office, Caden walked the short distance to Celeste's door, and poking his head in he requested a favor. She happily obliged, then striding to the foyer, he grabbed a community raincoat from the closet, and stepping outside he jumped into the golf cart sitting under the shelter of the portico. As he headed to the barn, though the rain was bucketing down around him, he paid it no attention.

"Jane, you made a big mistake," he growled through clenched teeth. "You can try and mess with me, but you picked on the woman I love and one of my dearest friends. You're gonna be real sorry."

CHAPTER SIXTEEN

CADEN HAD MADE A QUICK stop at the barn, poking his head in on Valentino and Goliath to make sure they were all right, then drove the golf cart down the gravel lane to the grey and white cottage Richard had described. Like the others, it was a storybook house, but it had the added feature of a small front yard and a white picket fence. Pulling the golf cart under the only shelter he could find, a large, nearby, oak tree, he ran through the rain, jumped the fence, and standing under the porch overhang he banged on the front door.

"Who is it?"

"Jane, it's Caden."

"Go fuck yourself."

"Not physically possible," he replied banging again.

"I'm not opening the door. You can stand out in that horrible weather all day if you want, I don't give a shit."

"Jane, last request, open the door."

"Go ahead and kick it down," she railed. "I can have you arrested and sue your ass as well."

Shaking his head, Caden reached into his pocket, and courtesy of Celeste, he withdrew a key. Slipping it into the lock he slowly turned it and walked inside.

"What the fuck?" Jane exclaimed staring at him in shock.

She was standing in the middle of the living room, cardboard boxes on the coffee table in front of her. It was obvious she was in the middle of packing.

"I did ask nicely," Caden said calmly, closing the door behind him.

"You have no fucking right to be in here," she hissed."I know what you did," he said ignoring her comment and unbuttoning his raincoat.

"What do you mean?" she said warily, eyeing him like trapped prey.

"A video has come to light," he continued, tossing his wet coat over a chair.

"A video? Of what?"

"I should say, several videos, but the one I'm talkin' about shows what happened with you and Bridget this mornin.'"

"Excellent," she beamed. "I have proof that bitch pushed me off that mounting block. Thanks for the great news, you moron."

"Uh-huh. It also shows somethin' else."

"Stop with the head games, just fucking tell me."

"Happy to," he said moving closer. "After Heather Chadwick and her mother left and you thought you were alone, you broke into a very satisfied smile."

"What does that prove?" she growled sidling away from him as he neared.

"You set the whole thing up. Somehow you found out that Heather and Bridget had struck up a friendship, and you knew Heather would tell her about the lesson, the one you managed to book by manipulating her mother."

"So what?"

"Sending Bridget off on a trail ride early, so she'd wonder why you wanted her outta the way, that was the bait. You knew her curiosity would get the better of her and she'd come back. You timed it perfectly. Bridget went crazy, just as you wanted her to. She'd be fired, and you'd have your petty victory, but it worked out even better than you'd planned, didn't it Jane?"

"Yeah," she said haughtily, "it did. I didn't expect her to get physical, but now I've got my ticket to a nice big settlement check, but you, Caden, you're a double moron. I had that horse sold to that Chadwick woman for a ton of money. You would've made a mint."

"The horse isn't for sale, period," he said shaking his head. "You have yet to learn that there are things in this life you can't put a price on."

"Oh, please," she said rolling her eyes. "You can leave now. You've told me you figured it out, big deal, now piss off."

"Not quite yet," he said soberly. "You also staged that scene with Tim to make him think you were pissed about Bridget's behavior, but you weren't. That was just another way to cover your tracks."

"Yeah, so what? It doesn't change anything. I'm in the middle of packing and I have zero interest in anything you have to say. You're wasting your breath. Like I said, piss off."

Stepping forward, she bent over to lift up one of the boxes on the coffee table, and Caden broke into a smile. It was the moment for which he'd been waiting. Reaching behind his waist he withdrew the long, thin riding crop he'd picked up at the barn. Moving silently behind her, he swished it across her seat with considerable force.

"Aaargh! What the fuck?"

Hands flying to her cheeks, she spun around, glaring at him in shock.

"I'll whip your ass 'til it's striped like a zebra if that's what it takes for you to pay attention," he declared. His voice was even, almost quiet, and his blue eyes carried a steely glint. "You understand me?"

"You bastard," she quivered, her brow crinkling as she glowered at him.

"Do you understand me?" he slowly repeated, locking her stupefied gaze.

Wordlessly she nodded her head, though she was still trying to make sense of what had just happened.

"Sit down," he said sternly.

Backing away from him, still gripping her stinging cheeks, she found the couch, and winced as her bottom touched the cushion. He was a few steps behind her, and lifting one foot on to the coffee table, he leaned his elbow on his raised knee and scowled down at her.

"You listenin', or is your ass stingin' so bad it's makin' it hard to focus."

"I'm listening," she breathed dropping her eyes.

"Hey," he said tapping the crop on her thigh, "don't be lookin' anywhere except at me."

Lifting her gaze she stared back at him.

"I'm still seein' so much arrogance in you. If I didn't have Bridget in my life, I'd find a way to spank your butt every single day until you started behavin' like a human bein.'"

"I, uh, don't know what you mean."

"Bullshit," he growled. "You know exactly who you are. That's why you're so good at what you do. You're a lyin', schemin' nasty girl, and I'll bet it's a rare thing for someone to call you on your crap."

"Fine," she said dropping her shoulders. "I admit it. It's how I am because it's the only way to get ahead in this world. Haven't you ever heard the phrase, nice guys finish last? The same is true for nice girls."

"There you go. That's the Jane I need to be dealin' with, the real Jane."

"What do you want?"

"You're not gonna be suin' anyone."

"The hell I'm not," she spat.

"You have two talents. You're not a horse person, not even close, but you're a damn good rider and you can manage a stable. I knew the first five minutes I saw you in the barn that you knew what you're doin."

"Yeah, so?"

"That's your first talent. Your second talent is that you can read people and use their weaknesses against them. Bridget's not stupid, but you were one step ahead of her the whole time. Even if she hadn't come back, you still would have gotten what you wanted. Not everythin', but you would have ridden Valentino, and won over Heather and her mother."

"Fine, yes, you're right, but get to the point. You still haven't told me why I'm not going to sue Richard and your precious Bridget, and get a shitload of money."

"Do you have any idea how long it takes to file and win a lawsuit, and the deep pockets you need? That video can be deleted in two seconds, and I can promise you, Heather and her mother will not support you. That means it's just your word against Bridget's, and Jane, that's not enough, not by a long shot, and that's just for starters."

"Fuck," she muttered. "I know where you're going next."

"Really? Tell me, let's see if you're as clever as I think you are."

"You know a zillion people in the horse world, and you have a spotless reputation. Everyone loves you. You'll spread the word that Jane Walters is a liability, and I won't be able to get a job doing anything but mucking shit."

"Not even muckin' shit," Caden said gravely. "I'll also get the word out to all my buddies who have sale barns, tellin' them to steer clear of any horse flesh represented by you. It might take me a month, six months, a year, but I will ruin you in the horse world, and do it happily. If you wanna go ahead and harass the people I love by messin' with 'em, go ahead, but believe me, Jane, you're gonna come out the loser, big time. How's your ass?"

"How do you think?" she snapped.

"Imagine if I whipped it like that a dozen, then two dozen, then three dozen times. That's how you're gonna feel if you go ahead with your nasty little lawsuits. You'll feel like I'm wailing my crop on your backside every time you turn around. Your name will be dirtier than mud."

"Okay, okay," she exclaimed throwing up her hands. "You win. I get it. No lawsuits. You can back off. I'm moving to Montana anyway. I've got a friend up there who's starting up a barn. I know he'll hire me."

"Yep, I'll just bet you do, and I hope he smacks your ass. That's what you need, along with some other things."

"In your dreams," she growled.

"Nope, there's only one girl in my dreams, and it sure as hell isn't you. I'm gonna leave this crop here, and if you start havin' second thoughts, you just take a real good look at it."

"I told you, you don't have to worry. You say I'm smart, well, I am, and I know when to cut my losses and move on."

Straightening up, he dropped the crop on the coffee table.

"Take it anyway," he said. "Maybe lookin' at it now and then might remind you that nice girls, and good people, don't always finish last."

A sudden peal of thunder echoed over their heads, and a flash of lightening crackled is brilliance through the small house.

"See, God agrees with me," he remarked as he moved across the room and pulled on his raincoat.

"Caden?"

"Yep?" he asked walking to the door.

"It wasn't personal."

"Never thought it was, at least, not to you," he replied. "Try usin' that brain for somethin' positive. What you get out of it might surprise you."

Opening the door he stepped out into the weather, and jogging over to the golf cart, which had become completely soaked, he settled in and started back to the house. The relentless rain saw him drenched by the time he reached the shelter of the portico and stopped at the front door. Taking off the coat and shaking it quickly, he stepped inside and hung it on the coat hook, then pulling off his wet boots, he left them by the front door and headed to Richard's office. Knocking on his door, he heard Richard's call to enter and stepped inside.

"How many times...?"

"I know," Caden said grinning, "I don't have to knock."

"Why are you in your socks?"

"Boots are soaked through. I didn't wanna walk 'em over your perfect floors."

"My staff thanks you," Richard said with a small bow of his head. "Do you bring good news?"

"I do, you don't have to worry about any lawsuits from your former employee."

"Seriously? I can't believe it. She was positively vile on the phone this morning. How did you manage that?"

"I gave her a reality check."

"I owe you," Richard sighed. "I truly owe you."

"Hey, I owed you walkin' in here a few days ago. Bringin' Bridget on board like you did, just so I had a chance to make things right, that was a big deal."

"Happy to do it, you know I'm a romantic at heart."

"Yeah, I do, so why don't you get outta that chair of yours and get with the program?"

"What? What do mean?" Richard mumbled as a pink blush crossed his face.

"That woman down the hallway that you can't do without! You think she's here just 'cos she likes the food?"

"I, uh, I..."

"Just sayin'," Caden said with a wink. "Ya know, when a cowboy loves a woman...!"

"When a cowboy loves a woman—what? Give me an end to that sentence."

"I'll say this much," Caden chuckled. "This cowboy is goin' up to his girl and he's gonna show her how much he loves her. What is a one time, corporate executive, ivy-league educated, dapper dan gonna do?"

Moving quickly to the door, leaving his speechless friend to ponder, Caden strode down the hallway and trotted up the stairs into his suite. Moving directly to his bedroom, he gazed lovingly at his sleeping Bridget as he stripped off his clothes and climbed gently into bed. He was tired, but that's not why he'd slipped between the sheets. He just wanted to be with her, and as he closed his eyes he let out a long, deep sigh.

Damn, this has been one helluva a day. I feel like I've just been bucked off a bronc that tried to break my back.

She moved an arm, dropping it against him, and turning on his side he looked across at her wounded, but peaceful face.

"I'm gonna spend my life makin' you happy," he whispered. "I'm gonna love you, and protect you, and spank your butt whenever you need it."

"You are?" she breathed without opening her eyes.

"I thought you were sleepin'."

"I am."

"I've got somethin' special waitin' for you at my ranch, and I'm gonna be takin' you there real soon."

"Caden, I remember what happened."

"You do?"

"You won't believe me."

"Of course I will."

"Promise?"

"I promise."

"Valentino saved my life, but I'll tell you how later. I need to keep sleeping."

"Okay, darlin'."

"Please stay here."

"There's nowhere else I wanna be," he sighed.

A shiver rattled down his spine. His hair was wet, and he realized he was chilled. Moving closer, snuggling into her body, he breathed in her warmth and sank into her energy. Moments later his eyes began to close, and the mattress summoned him to rest.

It was in the dark hours of the early morning when he felt Bridget's fingers gently wrap around his cock, rousing him from sleep. He was on his side, his back to her, and quietly groaning he rolled over and buried his lips in her neck. The soft smooth skin invited his tongue, and his hands began roaming leisurely over her body.

"Are you sure you're okay?" he whispered raising his head, his eyes falling on her grazed face.

"When I'm with you, I'm always okay," she breathed.

"I don't wanna hurt you."

"You won't, and if you do, I don't care."

Her hand returned to his manhood, gently massaging, and surrendering to their mutual need he pushed the covers away, then lowered his lips to her breasts. He could hear the splattering of rain against the windows, but it was an even, consistent drumming, almost a soothing melody, and devouring her nipples he felt his cock surge to life.

Dropping his fingers between her legs, he softly circled her clit, then applying pressure, he fervently rubbed, eliciting gasps of pleasure. Keeping his thumb against her nub, he thrust his middle finger into her depths, searching out the magic spot that would ripple its scintillating sensation through her body. Her cry told him he'd found it, and guided by her loud, needful moans, he touched and released several times before slowly withdrawing and sliding on top of her.

Kissing her gently, he snaked his cock home, and with slow, measured strokes, he brought her close to the edge, then whispering in her ear he pushed her forward.

"In my house," he breathed, "I have a special place reserved for you, a place that you will come to ache for, a place that will make you quiver, and beg and-"

"Please," she bleated, "I need to come."

"A place that will take you higher than you can imagine," he finished as he slowed, drawing out the moment.

"Caden, I'm begging, I'm right there, please, Sir."

"There you go," he whispered, "a please, Sir will usually get you want you want."

Rising up, gripping her hips, he surged forward, thrusting with powerful, rapid strokes. Her body grew taut as she toppled headlong into her moment, and as his cock jerked his eruption, he groaned his joy, uniting with her passionate wails. Moments later, resting in his arms, she murmured his name.

"Yes, darlin'?" he whispered.

"Thank you for making all this happen," she sighed. "Bringing me here. Bringing us back to each other."

As he felt her drift back to sleep, he had an unexpected epiphany.

He didn't want see her every few nights, or every other night. He wanted her with him every night. He wanted to wake up next to her, and to see her smiling face over his dinner table.

"I'm gonna make that happen," he whispered. "I'm not sure how, but I will."

CHAPTER
SEVENTEEN

EARLY THE FOLLOWING morning Caden slipped softly from the bed, showered and dressed, then kissing her on the unmarred cheek, he left a note on his pillow. The kiss was a vague whisper in her sleep, and late that morning when she finally woke up, it was because the phone was ringing on the bedside table. Glancing at the clock she was shocked when she saw the time, and with a deep yawn she picked up the receiver.

"Hello," she murmured.

"Bridget, it's Heather. I'm so, so, so sorry, are you okay?"

"Hi, Heather, yes, sort of."

"May I stop by? I have news."

"Do you care if I'm in my bathrobe?"

"Of course not, but if you'd rather wait-"

"No, I'd love to see you. Give me five minutes."

"Great, see you soon."

As Bridget hung up the phone and began to stretch, she saw the folded piece of paper waiting for her on Caden's pillow, and opening it up, she smiled.

Had an errand to run for my favorite girl. Back soon. xxx C.

Smiling happily, she was about to climb out of bed when she realized how hungry she was. Calling the kitchen she ordered a full breakfast, then placing her feet on the floor she carefully stood up. Her body was stiff and sore, and moving slowly into the bathroom, she lifted her eyes to the mirror to study her injuries. One side of her face was heavily grazed, and the orange salve the doctor had applied made it look even worse.

Dampening a cloth she moved it over the clear side of her face, gently over both eyes, then ran a comb through her hair, but not having been properly washed and conditioned, and dunked in a tub of bath gel, she could do nothing with it. Letting it fall in a disheveled mess around her shoulders, she lifted the bathrobe from the hook behind the door, wrapped it around her body and moved back into the bedroom.

"Do I have time to get dressed? Do I even want to?" she muttered.

A loud knock answered her question.

"Prepare yourself," she called as she shuffled through the living room. "I look like I'm wearing a halloween mask."

"I'm prepared," Heather called back, but as Bridget slowly opened the door, and Heather caught sight of her, she let out a gasp. "Oh, my, gosh, Bridget, I thought you said you were all right. You're not all right."

"It looks worse than it is," Bridget replied closing the door behind her. "It's all superficial. I can't say it doesn't hurt, but the doc said in a couple of days it will start disappearing. Children won't run screaming into the streets when they see me."

"This is all my fault," Heather lamented. "I'm so sorry."

"Don't be ridiculous," Bridget replied dropping down on the couch. "Jane is a righteous cow. She knew Valentino was off limits. I still don't understand why she did it. Anyway, tell me your news. I would love to talk about something besides Jane and the drama."

"Are you sure?"

"Absolutely positive," Bridget assured her.

"I took your advice. I called Jeff and asked him to tell me his side of the story. Bridget, you won't believe it. You were right. My mother cooked up the whole thing."

"She did? Good grief. Tell me everything."

"Jeff went to meet a reporter from Edge, you know, the music magazine. He was sitting at the hotel bar having a drink, and the next thing he knew, he woke up by himself in one of the rooms. It wasn't until he got my email that he knew what had happened."

"Oh, Heather, that's crazy, but how do you know your mother was behind it?"

"He managed to get hold of the hotel security camera footage. It showed him being helped from the elevator by two guys. The girl in the picture and my mother were walking behind them."

"Have you seen it?"

"No, but Jeff's bringing it with him."

"He's coming here?"

"Yes, and I can't wait. He'll be arriving any time now. When I confronted my mother she admitted everything, she had no choice. We had a huge fight, and she raved on and on about how she'd done it all because she loves me so much. This all happened yesterday, but because of the storm she had to stay overnight. She left earlier this morning."

"As incredible as this is, I'm honestly not surprised," Bridget remarked. "None of it made sense. I just find it hard to believe your mother thought she could pull it off."

"She was pulling it off, until I talked to you," Heather exclaimed. "She's a very determined woman. Some of the things she did to push my career would make a heck of a book."

"Maybe you should write it one day."

"You know, I think perhaps I just might do that, but regardless, I owe you."

"You don't owe me anything," Bridget said warmly. "Jeff would have found a way to reach you."

"It's more than that," Heather said quietly. "You've treated me like a regular person. Most everyone is weird around me. You don't know what it's like."

"Heather..."

"It's hard being me sometimes," she murmured fighting back the tears.

"You've been on an emotional roller coaster ride, and I know how that feels," Bridget said putting an arm around her shoulder, "but having to deal with all the publicity, and the stresses of your life, my gosh, I can't even imagine it."

"It's been very difficult," Heather whispered. "When I was down at the barn with you and Valentino, I felt different, like...this is going to sound odd, but...I felt like me. I must get back into riding. I miss it. I love horses, I love how they smell, I love their big brown eyes. Do you think I could have that lesson when you feel better?"

"You bet. I'll put you on a nice, safe, quiet horse and see where you're at, and we can take it from there."

"Thank you. I hope we can stay in touch after we both leave here."

"I'd like that, very much," Bridget nodded.

"I'd better get going. I want to make myself beautiful for Jeff."

"You are beautiful, and I don't mean just how you look. You and Jeff will be just fine. He sounds a bit like a cowboy."

"What do you mean?"

"When a cowboy loves a woman...! That's what Caden told me."

"When a cowboy loves a woman, what?" Heather asked.

"He won't tell me, but I get the drift."

"How about, when a cowboy loves a woman, she knows it," Heather suggested.

"Oh, my, gosh, I love that," Bridget declared.

"Jeff is sort of a cowboy," Heather said thoughtfully. "He's from Montana, and he's big into horses. He wants to buy a ranch there."

"Now I know you're in good hands," Bridget laughed. "Call me."

"You call me too, and I hope you feel better fast," Heather said rising to her feet.

"I will. Give me a week and I'll be a hundred percent, and was that a knock? Thank goodness, my breakfast is here. I'm starving."

"I'll let him in on my way out," Heather smiled, and walking briskly across the room she opened the door, stepping aside as the waiter rolled the cart into the room. "Bye, Bridget" she called with a wave.

"Bye, Heather," Bridget called back, slowly rising to her feet.

Moving across to the table she signed the room service check, then sat down and stared out the window. The storm had left evidence of its passing, but the sun was shining, and Tim and the grooms were hand walking the horses, waiting until the paddocks dried out before putting them back.

"Everyone has heard about what happened," the waiter said. "Just so you know, none of us cared for Jane."

"Thanks, Brian," she replied catching his name from his tag. "That's very sweet of you."

"In case you weren't aware, she's gone. She took off early this morning."

"Really?"

"Really. Anyway, enjoy your breakfast. I hope you heal up soon."

"Thanks. I'll be back in my little cottage in a day or two. I think Caden only has this suite for that long."

"Enjoy it while you can."

"Thanks, Brian. I intend to," she grinned.

Settling down she began to eat, and was almost finished when the door opened and Caden walked in with a wide smile.

"You're up," he declared. "How do you feel?"

"Better now that I've had something to eat," she replied. "I felt shaky when I got out of bed. What have you been up to?"

"Coffee," he replied.

"You've been up to coffee?" she laughed.

"Funny," he chuckled kissing her on the unscratched side of her face before sitting down. "I've been very busy, but before I tell you about that, you said you remembered what happened to you."

"I do. I don't know what took me so long."

"Shock," he replied pouring himself his much wanted coffee. "You were in a bad way when I found you. So, tell me."

"When I was passing that trail that led into the rocky area, do you know where I mean?"

"Yep, I know exactly."

"I stopped to look at it. I had no intention of going down there, it seemed treacherous, but there was a formation that caught my eye. It was an odd shape, and as I was staring at it, it moved."

"The formation moved?"

"It was a mountain lion."

"Bridget!"

"It was the way the clouds and sun were causing strange shadows, he'd blended into the rocks. Needless to say, I immediately pushed Valentino forward, but I was worried. When I turned on to the trail that looped around to bring me back, I kept looking over my shoulder. I was sure he was around, but I didn't see anything, then we reached the trees."

"You thought it would give you cover."

"Yes. I felt so exposed on the side of the hill like that, and I figured I could find my way through the trees and hit the trail on the other side. We'd gone in a little way when Valentino started to get spooky, so I got off. I thought it would be safer to lead him. I'd just hit the ground when I saw why he'd gotten so edgy."

"The lion?"

"The lion," Bridget nodded, her eyes wide. "I was so scared, Caden. He was about thirty, maybe forty feet away, and he started coming towards us. Valentino spun around and reared up, and when he did I jumped backwards and fell against a tree. I hit my head so hard, I swear, I saw stars, and I remember sliding down the trunk, grabbing it trying to hold on, then suddenly I was rolling. Of course that thicket is on a slope, it's not steep, but it's still a slope. I remember everything going black. Then I was dreaming about swimming in a lake and I couldn't get back to shore. I heard your voice and opened my eyes, and you were there."

"Valentino was standin' over you, guardin' you," he said quietly, shaking his head. "Damn."

"Horses are prey," Bridget frowned. "Why didn't he run?"

"His desire to protect you must have been stronger. That's just amazin'. I've heard of horses doin' things like that, but I took the tales with a grain of salt."

"I wasn't exaggerating when I said he saved my life."

"No, darlin', you weren't."

"That horse, I love him to bits," she murmured. "I was crazy about him from the moment I saw him."

"Like he was about you," Caden smiled, "and that brings me to one of the things I did this mornin'. I was able to reach Melinda."

"Because?" she asked, her heart skipping a beat.

"As of about, let's see, about thirty minutes ago, Valentino belongs to you."

"He does not!"

"He does," Caden nodded.

"But, doesn't she want a lot of money for him?"

"I worked all that out. Her biggest worry was findin' someone who would love him the way she did, and I was able to assure her that you would, and you do. I also reiterated that she could visit any time she wanted."

"Caden," she breathed, "I can't believe it."

"Believe it," he nodded. "I thought you'd like that better than flowers."

"What?"

"Richard suggested I buy you flowers and chocolates."

"No, Valentino is much better," she laughed.

"Are you ready for more?"

"I'm not sure. I'm kind of blown away right now, but go ahead."

"Uh, Bridget," he said leaning forward. "I'd love it if you'd come and stay at the ranch with me. Give it a try. The two of us."

"Oh, my, gosh! Caden."

"Whatta ya say?"

"I, uh, well, I'd have to work somewhere, somehow, but uh, yes, I would love that," she beamed.

"How would you feel about bein' the official trainer here. Tim has no interest in teachin'."

"So, I'd be living at your ranch, and drive here when a lesson is booked."

"Yep, and I promised Richard I'd find him another full time handler. One of my guys came down this mornin' to help right away, and he'll stay on until I do."

"Give up my place, and move to your ranch," she mumbled. "Don't you travel a lot?"

"Not as much as you think. I have my facility up near where you live, and I go back and forth between there and my ranch. Truth is, I was up your way a lot 'cos of you. I'd miss you when I'd come back."

"I'd miss you too. I hated it when you'd leave."

"You'll love the ranch, Bridget. You can help me with my babies, and show the horses when buyers come out. You're so good! I'd much rather you do the ridin', then I can do the sellin'."

"Sounds as if my time available for lessons here would be spotty," she remarked.

"Or you'll be real busy, which is good, it'll keep you outta trouble," he said with a wink. "I just wanna be with you," he said lowering his voice and carefully taking her injured hand. "I wanna wake up with you every mornin', and go to sleep with you every night."

"Caden, I feel the same. I've never lived on a ranch before, but as long as I'm with you, I don't care where I am."

"Is that a yes?"

"That's a yes," she whispered, swallowing back her happy tears.

"I wanna hug you real tight, but I know I've gotta be careful," he said standing up and taking her hand.

"Hug me as tight as you want," she sighed rising to her feet and leaning against him. "I'm so happy I want to cry, but I don't want to get my poor, scratched face all wet."

"You don't have to worry about that," he purred. "I'm gonna be here to dry your tears anytime you need me to. Seein' you on the ground like I did, damn, girl, it scared me so bad."

"You have no idea how I felt when I opened my eyes and saw you over me. You were, you are, my hero."

"Me and Valentino," he breathed.

"You and Valentino," she sighed.

Placing his finger under her chin he tilted up her head, and softly placing his mouth on hers, he glided and pressed, tickled with his tongue, skimmed his teeth over her lower lip, then gently suckled, until breathlessly she pulled back, and with sparkling eyes she silently begged him to take her. Sweeping her up he carried her into the bedroom, laid her down and opened her bathrobe.

"Close your eyes and don't you move," he said huskily.

She heard his footfalls take him into the bathroom, then the sound of the shower, and when he returned and laid next to her, slightly damp and smelling of spice, she caught her breath.

"Caden?"

"Yeah, darlin'?"

"Just hearing you come back turns me on."

Sliding his finger into her sex, his lips dropped to her ear.

"So I see," he mumbled. "When I get you home, you're gonna be wet like this all the time. Would you like to know why?"

"Uh-huh," she muttered as his fingers moved from her pussy to lightly pinch her nipples.

"Because part of your trainin' is to keep you wantin', and I'm gonna show you what I mean right now."

"You are?"

"I'm gonna stop in a minute, and just hold you, then start again, and I'm gonna do that for a while."

"Oh, Caden, you're making me crazy."

"At the ranch, when you're all healed up, I'll be doing more than just holdin' you."

"Like what?"

"Nope, that's all I'm gonna tell you for now," he crooned teasing her pussy, and slowly dropping his fingers away, he brought her into his arms.

"Cruel," she sighed.

"Yep."

"I love it so much."

"Yep."

"Will I be able to stand it?"

"Yep."

"How do you know?"

"Because, darlin', you won't have a choice."

An hour later, after tantalizing her body, driving her closer to the edge with every short, scintillating episode, he slid his cock into her soaking cunt and rode her to an explosive release. Lying in his arms, trying to catch her breath, she curled against him.

"You're wrong," she said breathlessly.

"I am? About what, darlin?"

"I won't be able to stand it."

"I guess we'll be findin' out pretty soon," he chuckled. "I'm thinkin' we should pack up Valentino and head off tomorrow."

"I'll hate to leave all this luxury," she sighed, "The amazing food, the room service-"

"Yep," he said interrupting her, "it's sure a nice place to spend some time, and we can always come back when it's not real busy here, but I have a feelin' you're gonna like the special amenities my place has."

"You know," she said with a wry smile, "I have the same feeling. I think I will too."

CHAPTER EIGHTEEN

EARLY THE FOLLOWING afternoon, after accepting a lunch invitation from Heather and Jeff, Caden headed to Celeste's office to return the key to Jane's cottage, while Bridget returned to the suite to pick up her handbag. Their suitcases were already in the horse van down at the barn. All they had to do was load Valentino and they could leave. Approaching Celeste's door, he gave a little knock and walked in, and to his delight he saw a dozen red roses in a crystal glass vase, and a large box of unopened chocolates sitting on her desk.

"What's this?" he asked with a grin.

"Uh, from Richard," she said shyly.

"That old fox," he laughed. "I've already said my goodbyes to him, so I'll refrain from stickin' my head in to razz him."

"Please do," she begged. "I think sending me these things was very difficult. He hasn't been able to look me in the eye all day."

"He'll get there. He's just catchin' his breath," Caden assured her. "The key was a big help, thanks, Celeste. I'll be back soon."

Leaning over her desk he pecked her on the cheek, then walking back into the foyer he found Bridget waiting.

"Ready?"

"Yes," she nodded.

"Let's take the golf cart," he suggested. "You still need to take things easy."

"Please, I can walk to the barn," she scoffed.

"You either come in the golf cart, or I'll pick you up in the van on the way out."

"Fine," she sighed. "I'll come with you in the cart."

Five minutes later Caden was loading Valentino into the horse van, and with a last goodbye and thank you to Tim, he and Bridget set off for his ranch.

The day was idyllic. Spotty clouds and warm sunshine made the drive picturesque, and when Caden turned off the main road, driving through a small town much like the one near Dudley's Dude Ranch, it was a short distance to the tree lined lane leading up to his house.

If the appearance of Dudley's had surprised Bridget when she'd first seen it, Caden's house was equally startling. She'd thought it would be a sprawling, one level ranch home, but she was met by a two-story, log house with double-story front windows. A natural grey brick front patio, and a chimney made of the same stone, gave the home an elegant appearance, and glancing across at him she broke into a smile.

"Caden, this place is gorgeous."

"Thanks. I've always had a thing for log cabins, but I wanted a decent-sized house that had a bit more appeal than just four square walls."

"It sure has that," she exclaimed. "When I first met you, didn't you describe yourself as a cowboy who sells a few horses, and trains a few more?"

"That's who I am," he winked.

"You don't have a home like that selling a few horses, Caden."

"I didn't have to buy the land," he replied. "It was my dads, I just-"

"You just built a phenomenal house and created a super successful horse sales and training farm is what you did."

"With a little help from my friends, as Joe Cocker once said. You know who he is?"

"Yes, I do," she nodded. "You are a very impressive man, Caden Price."

"Jane must have found out about this place," he remarked. "That's probably the only reason she was so aggressive."

"I doubt it," Bridget murmured leaning across the console. "You are one sexy cowboy."

"Sit back in your seat please, young lady."

"Spoilsport," she quipped.

As he continued down a gravel road, two large barns came into view, and he rolled the van to a stop.

"Where is everyone?"

"Probably out checkin' fencin' or workin' some horses in the ring."

"Where's it, the ring I mean?"

"Over there," he replied pointing to a building that appeared to be an oversized barn.

"But, that's huge."

"We need huge. Remember, this is a trainin' and sales barn, and in the winter we can't stop 'cos there's snow on the ground."

"I can't wait to see it," she said excitedly.

"You look like your feelin' better," he remarked.

"Change of scenery maybe. I'm still hurting, but I'm so happy it's probably overriding not feeling good."

"Let's get your boy outta the van and into his paddock, then I have someone who's been waitin' to meet you."

It only took a few minutes to unload Valentino, and as he descended the ramp he whinnied loudly, his nose in the air and his ears pricked.

"They remember him," Bridget declared as the horses in the nearby paddocks whinnied their response.

"He was here for several weeks, and horses don't forget," Caden said as they began walking him towards a group of fenced paddocks.

"How many horses do you have?"

"We've got almost forty right now, all levels of trainin', many here to sell. There are five full-time handlers, and the maintenance workers.

It's not a small operation, but it's at the point where it kinda runs itself. I mean, everyone knows their job and they do it."

"What do you do?"

"Me? I sell. Correction, I ride and sell," he said stopping at one of the smaller paddocks. "He's gotta be in a pasture by himself for a few days, until I decide who to put him with him. The horses he was with before have been moved."

"Of course, I understand," Bridget replied as she removed his halter and watched her stunning chestnut dance and prance and become reacquainted with his friends. "This feels really good, being here with you."

"Yeah, it does. I knew it would," he smiled. "Come with me. Like I said, I have someone I want you to meet."

They walked across a wide driveway to the first of the two large barns, and entering the wide aisle, Bridget saw several horses poke their heads out over their stalls doors.

"These guys are in here 'cos they're bein' worked, or have just been worked, or they're still bein' evaluated," Caden explained.

"I've never seen a barn this big," Bridget declared.

"I don't leave my horses out in storms, they come in, and I have to have enough room. Here we are," he announced pulling open a stall door.

Moving beside him, Bridget peered inside and let out a low, soft whimper. A foal was moving around the oversized stall on spindly legs, his mother paying close attention.

"Ooh, Caden, she's absolutely adorable."

"Remember, you have to name her."

"I feel so honored."

"We'll start imprintin' soon. You know about that, of course."

"Yes, of course, you touch her and handle her and let her know we humans are good people."

"Yeah, basically," he chuckled.

"Wow. I'm totally blown away."

She stood staring, falling in love with the sweet, baby foal in front of her.

"Caden, if I name her, you know what that means, don't you?"

"Uh, maybe not. Tell me."

"You can never sell her. In fact, don't show me any foal you're going to raise and train and sell."

"Oh, Lord," he laughed. "We're gonna have a problem with that one. I'm real careful about who buys my horses, I promise."

"I believe you, but you can't sell this baby. Not if I name her."

"Then I guess you own two horses now," he grinned.

"No, I own Valentino, this girl belongs to us both," she decreed.

"Come here you gorgeous thing," he muttered pulling her into his arms, but as he did, he felt her wince and relaxed his hold.

"For the next few days the only thing you're gonna be doin' is gettin' healed up," he said firmly. "You need to be takin' it easy and lettin' your body mend itself, you hear me?"

"Yes, Caden, and you won't get any argument from me. Yesterday was a month rolled into a few hours, and all of a sudden I don't feel right."

"Let's get you up to the house and settle you in."

"That sounds good. I suppose it was because this morning was kind of hectic, but I'm feeling super tired. Strange, it's just come over me out of nowhere."

"There's a gator here. I'll zip us up in that and stop at the van to grab our bags on the way."

"Yes, please," she sighed. "I was feeling so good until few minutes ago."

"That'll probably happen, a burst of energy then you'll flag," he said closing the stall door. "The gator's right through here."

The trip up the drive was a short one, but as they stopped in front of the house, Caden could see Bridget was grateful for the lift. Picking up the bags he walked slowly up the steps beside her, and unlocking the front door he ushered her in.

"You're pale," he said looking down at her.

"Yeah, I'm feeling pale," she said quietly.

"You feel like you're gonna pass out, don't you?"

"Uh-huh."

Putting down the bags, and effortlessly lifting her into his arms, he carried her up the stairs, down a short hallway and into his bedroom, laying her on his king-sized bed.

"Sorry," she muttered.

"We should have waited a couple of days before doin' this," he grumbled. "My fault, I'm sorry, darlin.'"

"Don't be sorry. I'm glad I'm here. It's so peaceful, and I'm not surrounded by drama and a ton of people."

"I'm gonna go make you some tea and get you somethin' to eat. Don't you move," he said shaking his finger at her.

"I couldn't even if I wanted to," she sighed, "which I don't."

"I'll be right back," he said softly.

He made his way down the stairs to the kitchen, and as he set the kettle to boil and popped some bread in the toaster, he thought about how happy he was to have her in his home.

"I'm gonna nurse you back to health, and I'm gonna take things real easy with you, but then, Bridget," he murmured, a grin crossing his lips, "I'm gonna open that special door, you're gonna walk down those stairs, and you're not gonna believe your eyes.

CHAPTER NINETEEN

Five Days Later

THE ONLY EVIDENCE OF Bridget's accident were faint lines that were already fading, her aches and pains were gone, and her energy had returned. Caden had been fanatical about her recovery, but his obsessive attention had restored her to full health.

It was mid afternoon. Caden had left the house after an early lunch, and Bridget had spent the afternoon hours arranging the storage of some of her larger belongings, and chatting to her friends, catching them up on all her exciting news. She was in the bedroom when she heard his footsteps climbing the stairs, and quickly ending her call, she darted into the bathroom to quickly run a brush through her hair and apply some lipstick.

"Hey, girl," he called.

"Caden, you're back," she said happily, stepping back into the bedroom.

"This is for you."

"Oh, how fun," she exclaimed looking at the large package he was carrying.

"Bridget," he said soberly, placing it on the bed. "Come here, darlin.'"

"Caden, you look so serious. Should I be worried?"

"Not at all," he said taking her hands, "not unless you've been naughty."

"No," she said feeling a stirring of butterflies.

"Do you remember what I said about your trainin'?"

She felt a shiver ripple through her body.

"Uh, yes."

"It starts right now. You call me, Sir, until I tell you otherwise."

"Yes, Sir."

"You change into what's in this box, and only what's in this box, then come on down to the livin' room. Kneel in front of the oversized easy chair by the fireplace, and you wait. Any questions?"

"No, Sir."

Leaning forward he pressed his lips on hers, his kiss fervent, his fingers around her hands tightening their grip.

"How do you feel?" he breathed.

"Nervous, excited, turned on," she whispered.

"Good. Remember, you kneel facin' the chair, and you wait," he repeated, then releasing her hands he strode from the room.

For a moment she stared at the package, then lifted the lid and pushed aside the tissue. Looking up at her was a paper thin, transparent white silk shirt, and lifting it out she marveled at its lightness. Pulling off her T-shirt and bra, she slid her arms down the sleeves and fastened the buttons. It was cool against her skin, immediately stiffening her nipples.

"Oh, man, this thing makes me feel so sexy," she mumbled.

Returning to the box she moved away the next layer of paper and found a pale pink, pleated skirt. As she lifted it up she saw it was as thin as the blouse, and short, very short, with an elastic waist. Peeling off her jeans and panties, she stepped into the skirt and pulled it up, then sitting on the bed she removed her socks.

"I feel naked," she muttered as she walked into the closet to look at herself in the full-length mirror. Staring at her reflection she could understand why Caden had chosen the scandalous attire.

It whispered across her skin as she moved, leaving goose bumps in its wake, and while her charms could be seen, they were more of a suggestion than blatant nudity. The outfit was salacious, but sensuous. Filled with anticipation, she headed down the stairs and into the living room.

The oversized picture windows that overlooked the driveway and hills beyond, had been treated with a reflective film. It not only conserved energy by keeping the house cool in the summer, it provided privacy. Those inside could look out, but those outside only saw a mirror reflection. Moving across the room to the large, natural rock fireplace, she noticed he had moved the thick, sheepskin rug in front of the chair, and as she knelt she could imagine how romantic the room would be in the winter. A blazing fire, snow outside, curled up with Caden and enjoying the comfortable intimacy.

She'd been waiting a few minutes when she sensed him behind her. There had been no sound of his footfalls, but she could feel his presence. Something touched the hem of her skirt, lifting it up to expose her bare bottom. She felt strangely self-conscious as the air touched her skin, and her fingers curled into her palms.

"Close your eyes. Hands behind your back."

His voice was deep and quiet, and feeling her butterflies spring into a frenzy, she did as he said, then held her breath. The skirt dropped, he was moving around her, then something tickled across her breasts, coming to rest on her nipples.

"If you get any spots or marks on those lovely new clothes, you'll receive a swat with a paddle. That's a swat for each. I'm very particular about certain things, Bridget, and I don't like stains on clothes, especially not those I've selected for you."

"I understand, Sir."

"I'm not sure you do. It's fine when you're ridin', it's expected, you can't be around horses and not get dirty, but in this house I expect you to behave like a lady, and dress like a lady."

Bridget had an unexpected flashback. He'd arrived in town unexpectedly and called her. It was late, but excited to see him she'd in-

vited him to stop by her apartment. She'd been wearing an old ki-
mono bathrobe when he'd knocked on her door, and she'd seen a dis-
approving frown as he'd walked in. She'd excused herself and hurriedly
changed.

"You've not always been so careful about your habits, but that won't
be acceptable here."

"Yes, Sir."

A sudden, hot sting sliced through her nipples.

"Aargh."

"No bra in the evening when we're in the house alone."

"Yes, Sir," she said breathlessly.

"Poor nipples," he purred moving his fingers over them to help ease
the pain. "Your bottom isn't the only area of your body that can be dis-
ciplined. Is my severity frightenin' you?"

"A little bit, Sir."

"Trainin' must be clear. If I'm not clear, I can't expect you to get
things right. I'll be strict, but I'll also be kind and lovin'. It goes together. Tomorrow you're gonna throw away any of your clothes that have
stains. Not your ridin' gear, that's different."

"Yes, Sir."

"After you've done that, you're gonna take a pen and paper and walk
through the house. If you see somethin' you'd like to change, or have
any suggestions for redecoratin', you make a note. I want you to feel like
this is your home, darlin',"

"Thank you, Sir."

"Shuffle around on your knees and drop on your elbows."

As she began to turn, she felt her face flame red, and she couldn't
understand why she was feeling so self-conscious. Taking a breath, she
slowly lowered herself on to her elbows, then caught her breath as her
skirt was flicked over her waist.

"Knees apart and arch your back."

Sliding her knees across the fur, she grit her teeth as his hands clasped her cheeks. She knew what was coming before it happened, but it didn't help her deep embarrassment when he separated them.

"I'm gonna start your trainin' back here," he said firmly, lightly touching her anus. "Don't worry, I'll take it slow, but it is gonna happen, and the sooner you accept it and surrender, the easier it'll be, and the faster you'll enjoy the pleasure it offers. Understand?"

"Yes, Sir."

"Stay there, just like that. I'll be back in a minute."

Kneeling as she was, her bottom exposed in the bright light of the living room, she felt a strange sensation, but it wasn't unpleasant. Quite the opposite. She hadn't fantasized about such an event, but it was unfolding like an erotic mystery, and as much as she dreaded the promised back door training, she couldn't deny there was a part of her that was tantalized by his lascivious promise. A few minutes later, as she heard him striding towards her, convinced he was going to start probing and touching her, she readied herself.

"Kneel up and shuffle back to face the chair. You may open your eyes when you're in position."

Surprised, she did as he directed, and when she was settled with her hands behind her back, she lifted her eyes and gazed up at him. His handsome face was softly smiling, and she saw nothing but love in his soft, blue-eyed gaze.

"This is for you," he said holding up a white leather collar. "This is the first collar, and as you progress you'll receive collars of a different color. Pink comes next, then red, and so on. Every time I give you a new collar, you'll also get a special gift."

"Sir," she breathed. "I didn't expect anything like this."

"There's no reason you should," he said as he placed it around her neck and buckled it closed. "There. Beautiful. How does it make you feel?"

"Wonderful," she sighed, "and I want the other collars. May I ask, what color is the last one?"

"The last one you'll see in a few minutes."

"Is this a common thing?"

"I'll explain more about the collars as time goes by. Enough talking. It's time to take you to my special place. A place where you will learn. Up on your feet and follow me, two steps back, hands locked behind you, eyes down."

Taking his hand, she slowly stood up. Her heart was pounding and her butterflies were quivering as he led her through the dining room and down the back hall. Stopping at a door, he pushed down the handle, opened it up and flicked on a switch. She saw a red glow, and her mind immediately took her back to her dream.

Oh, my gosh, the red room. It can't be, can it?

"Be careful, watch where you're walkin.'"

A white line showed the edge of each step, and as the door swung shut behind her, she heard the click of a lock.

"You don't have to worry," he continued. "This room is soundproof, and no-one can get in."

Her eyes adjusted to the dim light, and as she descended, and the room and its contents came into view, she let out a small cry.

"Sir, what is this?"

"Exactly what you think it is," he replied, "and I believe it's the room you saw in your dream."

CHAPTER TWENTY

FOLLOWING HIM ACROSS the thick, soft carpet, she gazed at the strange but fascinating furniture. Chairs with padded seats and odd arms, a low table with wide leather straps, a high, narrow bench hanging from the ceiling resembling a bizarre swing. Across the walls were closed cabinets, the contents of which she was almost afraid to imagine.

"Bridget," he said turning to face her, "is this the room you saw in your dream?"

"I only saw it for a minute, but it was all red, just like this. How did I know?" she breathed.

"I guess you glimpsed your future, darlin'. When you told me I could hardly believe it, but then I saw it as a validation of everythin' that's happened between us."

"I don't know what to say."

"I don't think you need to say anything, and now I'm gonna move on, in the room of your dreams."

"Oh, my goodness."

"The outfit you're wearin' is just one of many I'll give you. As your play wardrobe grows, I'll tell you which I want you to wear, but they are for my eyes only unless I tell you otherwise. You must keep them separate from your other clothes. This is beautiful on you," he said softly, reaching out his hand and squeezing her breast. "It makes you feel beautiful, doesn't it?"

"Yes, Sir," she whispered, "and very sexy."

"Clothes can be foreplay, for me they are foreplay, and I want you to see them that way too."

"Oh, Sir, I do.

"Sometimes I'll keep you in the same clothes for a couple of days. This is in the evenin's, of course, when it's just the two of us."

"Yes, Sir, I understand."

"When we come down here, though, the clothes come off," he said sternly. "Stay there."

Walking across to a counter he picked up a remote control, and a sensuous melody began echoing through the room.

"Strip. Make me want you."

Lifting her arms above her head she began to move to the music, swaying her hips and losing herself in the erotic display. Slowly unfastening the buttons, she let the shirt fall apart but didn't take it off, then languidly turning her back to him, continuing to move her hips, she gradually lowered her skirt over her backside and let it drop to the floor.

As the dance continued, and she started to turn back around, Caden swallowed a wave of heavy emotion. For years he had dreamed of bringing a special woman into his den of decadence, but every time he'd come close, something had gone awry. When he'd met Bridget, he'd sensed very early that she was *the one*. Now that his long-held desire was being realized, he could hardly grasp that it was truly happening.

He watched her last sensuous move as the shirt slipped away, and reaching down she picked the skirt off the floor, draped it over her arm with the blouse, and waited.

Pushing away the surge of heat that had exploded in the back of his throat, Caden ambled over to her, and reaching his hand behind her head, clutching her hair, he kissed her ardently, crushing her lips as his hunger surfaced.

"You are perfection," he muttered. "There's a chair at the base of the steps. Place the clothes there, then come back and stand where you are now, with your eyes closed and your hands behind your back."

"Yes, Sir," she replied breathlessly.

Her pulse was racing, and she could feel the hot, slick wetness between her legs. As she moved away she could feel his gaze following her, but when she deposited the clothes on the chair and turned back around, he was retrieving something from one of the cabinets. Returning quickly to the assigned spot in the middle of the room, she stared at the red carpet beneath her feet before closing her eyes. It looked just like the carpet in her dream.

He was right. I glimpsed my future.

"Feet apart," Caden directed as he approached.

Shuffling her feet, she held her breath as he walked behind her, but when the blindfold slipped over her eyes, she let out a long, soft breath.

"That's my girl," he purred as he began planting soft kisses on her neck. "Surrender to the pleasure."

His words floated around her like a warm breeze on a spring day, and when he took her elbow and led her forward, she had no trepidation, just an ache for whatever might come next.

"YOU'RE FACING A BENCH. It has padded extensions for your knees and elbows. Feel your way forward and take up the position you had in front of my chair in the living room. Don't worry, I'll guide you."

Reaching out in the dark, her sense of helplessness seemed to add to her carnal heat, and as he took hold of her limbs, helping her find her place, his sure, confident hands sparked through her skin.

"Sir," she whispered as she felt cuffs being placed around her thighs.

"Yes, darlin'?"

"I feel so..."

"So?"

"So much. There are no words," she murmured.

"I understand, darlin'. Sink into it. Take some deep breaths while I finish."

The leather around her legs was buckled, then her ankles and wrists, and she did as he said, taking long deep breaths as he went about his task.

"No talkin', but if things get too much, you yell out the word orange, like a traffic light. Understand?"

"Yes, Sir."

"If somethin' happens suddenly, like a cramp or you need me to stop right away, you yell out red."

"Yes, Sir."

Leaning down he kissed her cheek and stroked her hair, then moved around her body, relishing the sight of her bound and vulnerable. The position had her seat cheeks wide open, and her glistening, swollen pussy looked even more luscious in the hedonistic red light. To the sound of her soft moans he stroked her back and whispered his fingers across her inner thighs, finally touching between her needy sex. She wriggled as much as her shackles would allow, bleating for more, and he obliged her for a few minutes, circling her clit and thrusting his finger back and forth in her hungry channel until she was panting, but his attention was not because of her pleading, it was to heighten her arousal.

Reaching into his pocket, Caden withdrew a small, plastic bottle of lube, and squeezing a dollop on the tip of his finger, he smeared it across her dark hole. She let out a wail of protest, but he had expected nothing less, and standing beside her, placing one hand on the small of her back, he began to spank.

"You've haven't felt the heat of my hand since we left Dudley's" he declared as he continued to swat. "That's gonna change. I promised you I'd keep this bottom hot and tender, and I keep my promises. You're gonna be over my knee while I'm watchin' a football game, or I'll bend you over the kitchen island while you're cookin', and sometimes I'll spank you real good before you go to sleep. You got a problem with that, little girl?"

"No, Sir," she gasped.

"It won't always be hard, but it will be when necessary," he said without pausing his smacking palm. "Most of the time I'll just bring a nice sting to your ass, remind you to behave, or just 'cos I wanna see it turn a pretty shade of pink. That's how it's gonna be."

The more he talked, the more the sparks surged through her sex. His threats weren't frightening her, but fueling her hunger, until finally the need became so great she had to call out.

"Sir!"

"You need to say somethin'?" he asked dispatching his slaps to her sit spot.

"I, uh, just want you so much," she managed.

"You wouldn't be sayin' that just to get me to stop whalin' on your ass, would you?"

"No, Sir, no."

"Let's see," he muttered dropping his fingers into her sex. "Damn. I've never felt you so drenched."

"Sir, I want you so much," she repeated as he swirled his finger in her slick wetness.

"Uh-huh. If you're real obedient, and do as I ask, you'll get my cock and you'll get your release, but you know what I'm gonna do."

"Ooh, yes, Sir."

"If you resist, if you don't surrender like a good girl, I'll just have to spank you some more, and tease you for a while longer. The choice is yours. I'll let you think about it for a minute."

She heard him move away, then the sliding of a drawer, and his returning footfalls, soft on the thick carpet.

"Have you made up your mind?" he asked as he moved his hands over her hot, red seat.

"Yes, Sir. I'll behave."

"Good girl," he purred sliding his fingers into her crack.

She winced, but she didn't wriggle, and he let them rest there until he heard her let out a breath. Pulling the lube from his pocket, he picked up the small, hard rubber phallus he'd retrieved from his dildo drawer, and smeared it with several generous dollops.

"This is small, this is just to start your trainin'," he declared as he placed the tip against her. "Be a good girl now. Long deep breaths. Accept it, just let it slide in."

Bridget could feel it pressing, and though everything in her wanted to refuse, his coaxing, reassuring words enveloped her, and with a long deep breath, she surrendered.

"There you go, good girl, that's it. I'm real proud of you darlin'. I'm gonna press it just a bit further now."

As the dildo disappeared between her cheeks, his cock demanded to be released from the confines of his trousers, and stepping back, gazing at his success, he stripped off, rubbing himself for a brief moment before returning to her side.

"Just gonna move it a bit," he warned taking hold of the flange. "You're doin' real well."

During the few minutes he'd left her, Bridget had resigned herself to the unwelcome intruder, almost relaxing, and when he started to move it in and out, she let out a gasp, feeling the first glimpse of pleasure.

"There now," he purred withdrawing it completely, "that's a real good start. You still want my cock in your pussy?"

"Oh, yes, Sir, please, desperately," she wailed.

"You ever been fucked while restrained?"

"No, Sir, just the little bit that you did once or twice."

"It's a different feelin', darlin', and it's gonna make you come hard, real hard. You just release when you feel it," he said sliding into her slick, swollen pussy. "Next time, I'm gonna make you wait, so enjoy this."

Clutching her crimson cheeks he started to stroke, delighting in her immobility, moving with slow, forceful thrusts, then reaching underneath her, he tickled her clit, eliciting high pitched squeals between her heavy panting. As he accelerated, pumping with abandon, her moans and gasps told him her moment was almost upon her, and a second later she exploded.

Her shrieks didn't surprise him, but they sent him into his own release, and closing his eyes he groaned loudly, plunging his cock with renewed vigor. He didn't know for how long his climax lasted, but her cries ended with his, and he slipped from her depths, shriveled and spent.

Almost dizzy, he moved to a nearby shelf and picked up a small towel, and wiping himself, he carried it back to tend to her. She was softly whimpering, and as he unfastened the buckles, releasing her from the cuffs, she leaned into his arms as he helped her off the bench.

"This way," he purred leading her to a dark corner.

She'd not seen it, but nestled against the wall was a full-sized bed. Collapsing on top of it he pulled her into his arms, and in seconds they were both drifting into never-never land.

It was Bridget who was the first to move, and raising her head she stared up at his handsome face.

"That was shocking," she murmured.

"Which part," he asked sleepily.

"All of it. May I ask you something I probably shouldn't?"

"Sure," he said giving her a reassuring squeeze.

"Have you brought many women to this room?"

"Bridget," he said with a heavy sigh, "you're the first."

"You put together this amazing place and never brought anyone down here?"

"Nope. I've come close a few times, but it never seemed to work out. I've been waitin' my whole life for this, for what just happened."

"I'm speechless," she muttered.

"Me too. I think I just said all there is to say."

"I feel so..."

"I thought you said you were speechless."

"I am, but I feel so..."

"Special?" he asked, finally moving and propping himself up on an elbow.

"Yes," she breathed.

"Haven't you figured that out yet, darlin'? You are special. You'll always be special."

"To think I almost blew this because I jumped to some stupid conclusion," she said, shaking her head.

"I wasn't gonna let that happen," he said firmly. "Remember what I told you?"

"You mean, when a cowboy loves a woman...?"

"Yep."

"I think I know what it is now. When a cowboy loves a woman, she knows it!"

"That's close."

"It's close?"

"Yep. Real close."

"Caden, you have to tell me."

"Nope, but there is a small piece of unfinished business."

"There is?"

"Remember when I wouldn't let you touch yourself?"

"Yes, you were at the ranch and we were talking on the phone. Oh! I never did find out why you said no."

"Can you figure it out now?"

"Let me think," she said softly. "Oh, my, gosh, was it because I didn't say, please, Sir?"

"Yep, that was one of the reasons, the one you needed to get to," he replied. "You also needed to feel what it was like to obey me."

"Please, Sir," she sighed. "So simple, but so important."

"Yep. It means a lot, darlin'," he said softly. "Now it's time to get your beautiful red backside upstairs, but before we go I'm gonna show you somethin'. Stay there."

She watched him slip from the bed and move across to the cabinets, returning with a black velvet box.

"This is the last collar," he said soberly, sitting on the side of the bed. "Are you ready to see it?"

"Yes, Sir, please, I would love to."

Bridget stared, mesmerized as he lifted the lid, and as its contents came into view she caught her breath.

"Caden, it's exquisite."

A gold band with rolled edges stared up at her, and in the center, hanging from a sliver ring, in a silver setting, was a large, pear-shaped diamond surrounded by sapphires. Pulling her eyes from the jewels, she looked at the back, and saw a series of tiny plates.

"What's that?" she asked, pointing at it.

"The lock. Once it's in place it can only come off if I unlock it, and the teardrop in the center—that unclasps so a leash can snapped on the ring."

"Thank you, for showing me, Sir. It's, uh, very motivating."

Closing the lid, he returned it to the cabinet, then moving to the chair at the bottom of the stairs, he picked up her clothes and carried them back to her.

"Time to dress, darlin'. We're gonna shower, cuddle for a bit, then you're gonna make me dinner."

"Yes, Sir," she sighed. "May I wear an apron when I cook?"

"I'd sure advise it," he nodded.

A while later, after their shower and a short nap, Caden was about to move from the bed to get dressed, when Bridget took hold of his arm.

"Caden."

"Yes, darlin'?"

"When Heather decided to talk to Jeff, and the storm was coming in, she remembered something an old friend once said. A storm blows in change. There's the drama of the thunder and lightening, the rain to wash everything clean, and then the dawn of a new day."

"I like that," he murmured.

"I want to call the foal, Dawn."

"Bridget, that's perfect," he smiled.

"It's her, it's us, it's what has happened. Her birth signified the dawn of our life together, the dawn after all the drama, everything you did to..." then abruptly pausing, she crinkled her forehead. "Oh, my, gosh!" she exclaimed.

"What now?" Caden chuckled.

"I know the answer," she grinned.

"The answer to what?"

"When a cowboy loves a woman!"

"I'm listenin'."

"When a cowboy loves a woman, he makes sure she knows it."

"There you go," he grinned pulling her into his arms, "and if I ever don't, you have to tell me."

"All I have to do is look into your eyes to see it," she sighed.

"Then keep lookin' darlin', 'cos my love for you is always gonna be there."

THE END

DEAR Reader:

Thank you for buying this book. If you have a moment I would greatly appreciate your review. I constantly strive to bring you interesting and enjoyable content and your feedback is valued. Feel free to contact me at any time. I love to hear from readers. My email is: MagCarpenter@yahoo.com, and here are my social media links should you care to check them out.

My very best wishes,
Maggie

BOOKS BY MAGGIE CARPENTER

Cowboys
ROUGH COWBOY
HUNKS and HORSES
A Four Book Series
HEA - STANDALONE
(Featuring characters from COWBOY: His Ranch. His Rules. His Secrets)
TO KISS A COWBOY
TO CATCH A COWBOY
TO CON A COWBOY
TO TRUST A COWBOY
Sexy Scifi - Paranormal
ROUGH ALPHA
TRAINED BY THE ALIEN:
WARLOCK : THE ALIEN'S RULES:
BDSM Contemporary Romance
WET 1
WET 2
SINS BEHIND THE SCENES:
I AM A DOMINANT:
DESIRE UNLEASHED - Sexsomnia.
TIMELESS OBSESSION
For a full list of her novels visit her author page.
https://www.amazon.com/author/maggiecarpenter

About the Author

Award-winning and best-selling author Maggie Carpenter has published over fifty romance novels, and is the recipient of a number Spanking Romance Reviews awards spanning a variety of genres. Her readers describe her work as, romantic, funny, suspenseful, beyond a five-star read, exciting romance with a ton of surprises.

Her work includes a best-selling twelve-book contemporary cowboy series, Cowboys After Dark, (http://amzn.to/2ihCNtp), a warrior fantasy trilogy, Warriors After Dark, (http://amzn.to/2iE0cDa) contemporary love stories, and several Victorian romances. His Willful Bride was a #1 best-seller for several weeks and a BookBub Feature Deal. She is best known for her smart, witty, strong-willed women who bring unexpected challenge, mystery and humor into the lives of passionate, dominant men.

Maggie has a history in show-business both in front of and behind the camera, but moved from Los Angeles to live in the Pacific Northwest to pursue her writing. She is an equine enthusiast who rides every day, and writes until the wee hours of the morning when her eyes close only because they must.

This author loves to hear from readers. You can contact her through her website: www.MaggieCarpenter.com. To sample her work for free, go to, www.3FreeBooks.com.

Read more at https://www.MaggieCarpenter.com.